# Daddy's Temptation

## KELLY MYERS

Copyright © 2021

All rights reserved. No part of this publication may be reproduced, distributed, or transmitted in any form or by any means, including photocopying, recording, or other electronic or mechanical methods, without the prior written permission of the publisher, except in the case of brief quotations embodied in critical reviews and certain other non-commercial uses permitted by copyright law.

This is a work of fiction. While, as in all fiction, the literary perceptions and insights are based on life experiences and conclusions drawn from research, all names, characters, places and specific instances are products of the author's imagination and used fictitiously. No actual reference to any real person, living or dead, is intended or inferred.

# Blurb

**It's true. I attract trouble. I really do.**

**And this time, trouble stands before me in the form of a man I should be running away from.**

But instead, this is what I do.

I offer him my V-card.

Could you blame me?

I wanted to get rid of it after my uncle tried to sell it off.

Yes, that's what made me run away from Indiana.

Ryan is my best friend's dad.

A former military pilot.

And a man who is so droolworthy that I question my own sanity.

They call him "Foxy Flyboy."

And I just call him my biggest scandal ever.

Am I ready to deal with the consequences if he accepts my offer?

# Chapter One: Hailey

*Whew.* I let out a breath, drop the heavy box and swipe a strand of dark hair back off my sticky face. Leave it to me to move in August, the hottest damn month of the year. Although, I have to admit that the Southern California version of August is much drier than the humid one I just left back in Indiana.

*Good riddance.*

I've spent the last 23 years trapped in the Hoosier State and now I'm finally free. I throw my arms wide and look up at the blazing blue sky above. Los Angeles is going to be my salvation and I have big plans. But, first things first. I lean over, struggle to pick the box of books back up then decide to just kick them the rest of the way up the sidewalk and through my first-floor front door.

As I'm pushing the box along the pavement, my flip flop gets caught on the corner and I trip. "Dammit," I mumble. I bend over and slide the stubborn box forward. *Crap.* I think I just tore the bottom loose. I really should've hired movers, but I barely had enough money to get here. There's no way I could've justified such an extravagance.

"Need some help?" a deep voice asks from behind me.

I straighten up and turn to see an extremely handsome man standing there. I shield a hand over my eyes and look up. *Good Lord, he's tall.* "Um, sure. Thanks."

"You must be Hailey," he says and steps forward. "I'm Ryan Fox. We spoke on the phone."

"Oh, right. You're the owner of the building."

"And, manager. So, if you ever need anything, I'm right over there." He nods his dark head to the corner unit. "Apartment 7."

When the sunshine catches his eyes, I can't help but notice how green they look. Bright and a lighter shade that reminds me of mint chocolate chip ice cream. It's my favorite flavor and I'm not going to lie, Ryan Fox's eyes are pretty yummy-looking.

He picks up the box that I packed way too much in with ease and I force myself to look away. But, not before I see the muscles flex at the edge of his shirt sleeve. "Thanks," I say and lead the way toward my new place, apartment 12. He follows me inside and looks around. "Anywhere in particular you want this?"

"Oh, um, how about over there," I say and point to the corner. He walks over and sets the box down then steps back and dusts his hands off. "Sorry, it's so heavy, but all of my music books are in there."

"Music?"

"I'm a singer. I collect all sorts of coffee table books from Broadway musicals to biographies of musicians."

"That's cool. So, you moved out here to pursue a singing career?"

*One of the reasons,* I think. "Yep."

"Where are you from again?"

"The middle of nowhere pretty much. The Midwest is probably the most boring place in the entire country so I'm happy to leave it behind." I'm evading his question, but hopefully he doesn't really notice.

"Well, welcome to Sunset Terrace."

I decide that I love his voice. It's warm and velvety and reminds me of suede. I always notice people's voices since I sing. The timbre and pitch. The color and texture of someone's voice is a subtle, invisible thing that I have a knack for discerning. Not everyone can do it and it's not like any kind of science is involved. It's almost like asking someone to explain how one cloud differs from another.

Ryan has a voice that makes me want to wrap myself up in it. It's rich, soothing, deep and so very masculine. If his voice were a drink, it most definitely would be hot chocolate.

"Thanks," I say and study his face for a moment. He's good-looking, like really attractive, and I'm guessing he's near forty. Normally, I stay away from older men because of what happened with my uncle. But, Ryan doesn't scare me. Quite the opposite, in fact.

Ryan Fox intrigues the hell out of me. Something about him draws me in and I wonder if he's married. I glance down and don't see a ring.

"Anything else I can help you with?" he asks and places his hands on lean hips.

My head snaps up from his left hand. "Oh, no, I'm almost done," I say. "I'd offer you a bottle of water, but I don't have any yet."

The corner of his mouth edges up just the slightest bit. I notice he doesn't seem to smile much. At all, really. "No problem. It was just one box."

I watch him head back to the door and can't help but check out the way his jeans hug his ass. And, it's a mighty-fine ass. I may still be a virgin, but a girl notices these things. In fact, it's one of the reasons I left Indiana and moved to the big city. I want to find someone I actually like, preferably a man who is experienced, and will make it good for me. Because I came extremely close to having my virginity taken by a stranger.

Thanks to my good-for-nothing uncle. *Ugh.* The thought of my Uncle Wayne makes my stomach churn.

Ryan turns around at the door. "Oh, I have some paperwork for you to sign when you get a second. Just some lease stuff."

"Sure. I'll swing by in a bit."

"No rush," Ryan says. "Whenever you're settled, come on over. I'll be around."

I watch him disappear and lean against the wall, trying to get my rapid heartbeat under control. "Ryan Fox," I murmur. *Hmm.* He may be just the man for the job. The man who can introduce me to a whole new world of sensuality and the one I will give my virginity to. Just the thought makes me shiver.

I know people say you should wait. Wait until you're older, wait until you're ready, wait until you're in love. Ironically, everyone who preaches for you to wait have all had sex. I may not be in love, but I am 23 and I am beyond ready. From my experience, I know the best thing is to get rid of it as soon as possible when people like my Uncle Wayne think they can use it as a bargaining chip. But, I also want it to be with someone who will make it a good experience.

I shudder and walk back outside into the sunshine, hoping it will help warm my soul. Ever since my parents died in a car accident when I was sixteen, I've felt alone and unprotected. I went to live with my Aunt Sylvia and Uncle Wayne and things were alright for a while. But, when my Aunt Sylvia died last year, everything changed.

My Uncle Wayne changed.

I try to block out the bad memories and begin to hum a tune under my breath. Singing has been my solace, my safe place, and I use it to block out the pain and transport myself to another place. All I want to do is leave my old life behind and embrace my new life here in L.A.

"Hey, neighbor!"

I turn and see a gorgeous, long-legged girl with straight, silky, dark hair head my way. She has naturally tan, flawless skin and a worldly air about her.

"I'm Jasmine Torres," she says and offers a bright-white smile. "Welcome to the building."

"Thanks," I say, immediately loving her energy and enthusiasm. "I'm Hailey Lane."

"Nice to meet you." She glances over my shoulder and into my place. "Are y'all moved in yet?"

"Just about," I say and nod to the old pickup truck at the curb. "I have a couple more boxes."

"C'mon, I'll help," she offers and heads down the sidewalk.

We each grab a box out of the back and she looks down at the license plate. "Indiana, huh?" That was quite a drive."

"Sure was. I'm exhausted. You from here?" I ask.

She shakes her head. "Texas, originally. But, I moved here for modeling."

Yes, it is quite clear that Jasmine Torres is a model. She is probably almost six-feet tall with legs for days and a slim build that was made for clothing designers. She probably looks perfect no matter what she wears. Me, on the other hand...I look down at my 5'5" frame with a few too many curves. "What kind of modeling do you do?" I ask.

"I used to do all kinds, but now I only do runway. What about you? Did you move here to chase a dream like everybody else in this building?"

"I'm a singer. So, yeah."

We both laugh. "If you're serious, then this is the place to be. And, if you actually have some luck and talent then you'll make it."

We walk back into my place and set the boxes down.

"The girl who lived here before you-- Savannah-- was a model."

"Was?"

"She booked a couple huge campaigns, fell in love with her very hot photographer and the rest is history. Nick just moved her into his place in Malibu. Now she's studying to be a vet."

"Oh, nice." I look around my little place and, for the first time in my life, have something that's all mine. It feels good. "Well, I'm happy there was a vacancy because I think I'm really going to like living here."

Jasmine nods. "Sunset Terrace is great. Everyone here is really cool and there are a lot of people our age to hang out with. Every weekend, we have barbecues, swim and lay out. It's pretty chill and nice to unwind after work and traveling all week."

"Sounds fun."

"Well, I'll let you unpack," she says. "If you need anything, I'm right next door."

"Okay, thanks. I have to go sign some paperwork, anyway."

She gives me a sly smile. "Have you met Foxy Flyboy yet?"

I frown. "Who?"

"Ryan Fox, the owner/manager."

"Oh, yeah," I say and flush. "He helped me with a box earlier."

"Of course, he did," she says with a chuckle and rolls her eyes. "He's quite the gentleman and always looking out for everybody. Kind of like a father-figure to all of us here."

I just nod, remembering those striking green eyes of his. "Why do you call him Foxy Flyboy?"

"He used to fly planes or helicopters or something when he was in the military. And, well, his last name is Fox and, let's face it, the man is pretty damn hot."

I can't deny it. "Does he know you call him that?"

"Oh, hell no!" She bursts out laughing and I can't help but smile. "If he ever found out, he'd probably die of embarrassment. Ryan is a really nice guy, but he can be shy and mostly keeps to himself. God, I've lived here three years and never saw the man bring a woman back to his place."

"Really? So, he's not married?"

"Divorced, but no one knows any of the details. He's pretty close-mouthed about himself. He does have a daughter, but I don't think they talk much because she never comes around."

*A daughter? Oh, wow.* "How old is he?" I ask, trying not to sound too interested. But, I have to admit, I am extremely curious about him.

"Forty-three, I think."

Twenty years older than me. *Yikes*. That was a pretty big age gap. But, I kind of didn't care. I just need a nice man to step up and be my Mr. Right. Preferably someone as handsome as Ryan.

"He looks younger," I muse.

"Men," she says and rolls her dark, almond-shaped eyes. "They just get better with age. Lucky bastards." Then, she tosses me a wave and slips out the front door. "See 'ya later, Hailey!"

"Bye!"

Well, thanks to Jasmine, I just got the scoop on Ryan "Foxy Flyboy" Fox and it doesn't sound too bad. I don't usually date divorced men with daughters, but, then again, I'm not looking to get married. I just want one night full of pleasure to help me forget and make the nightmare of my uncle go away. I'm ready for my new life here to begin and I can't shed my old life fast enough.

# Chapter Two: Ryan

After helping the new tenant with the heavy box, I wander back to my corner apartment, pull my shirt off and stand in front of the air conditioning unit in the window. I tilt my head back and let the icy air blow on over my sticky chest and face, trying not to think too hard about Hailey Lane.

The girl is gorgeous, no doubt about it. And, she seems like a sweet kid. *That's right, Fox. A kid. Keep your mind out of the gutter.*

"Christ," I swear and drop my head between my shoulders, letting the cool air dry the sweat on my body. I haven't been interested in a woman in a long time and the first one I notice happens to be the same age as my daughter.

*Speaking of which…*

I give my head a shake and pull my cell phone from my back pocket. I pull up my favorites and there's only one name listed there. *Bella.* Unfortunately, I don't dial it too often because my daughter doesn't want much to do with me.

With a sigh, I begin to type a text to her. After debating what exactly to say and just how to say it, I finally settle on a message ten minutes later: *Hi, Bella-Vanilla. I just wanted to wish you a Happy 23rd Birthday. I'd love to catch up over lunch. Love you, Dad.*

Before I can think too hard about it, I hit send.

Bella is the most important thing in my pathetic life and she likes to pretend that I don't exist. I feel a stab of pain and set my phone down. I never planned on becoming a father at 20, but it happened and I tried to do the right thing so I married Paige.

I don't know if we were ever really in love. But, I knew I had a responsibility to help take care of the baby. My job wasn't great at the time and I'd always wanted to do something bigger and better with my life so I ended up joining the Army.

It didn't take long to see that I had a knack for flying. You know that scene in Top Gun where the jets take off and land on the aircraft carrier in the middle of the ocean? Yeah, that was me.

I had talent and was a damn good pilot so joining the 160th Special Operations Aviation Regiment (SOAR) was my goal. 160th SOAR soldiers, also known as Night Stalkers, fly classified missions using highly-modified Black Hawk, Chinook and Little Bird helicopters, among other things.

To be a Night Stalker pilot, I went through rigorous training to become mission-ready to fly in the most challenging conditions, including bad weather and enemy fire, all while relying on infrared and night-vision equipment to navigate through the darkness.

As a SOAR soldier, your ultimate goal is always to complete flight missions safely under pressure. Bad weather, enemy fire and tricky terrain are all secondary to the fact that your missions take place in the darkest part of the night.

Operating in the shadows, I was one of the elite pilots responsible for getting DELTA Force and Navy SEAL special operators into and out of some of the most secret and dangerous operations of the US military. We'd rather die than quit. Hence, our motto-- "Night Stalkers Don't Quit," often shortened to "NSDQ!"

It was an amazing, extremely dangerous job, but I felt like I was finally doing something worthwhile. Unfortunately, the shaky relationship I had with Paige crumbled since I was gone so much. We ended up divorcing after a few years and Paige took Bella while I immersed myself in my military career.

Over the years, I saw Bella when I could, but we were never very close. I always got the feeling that Paige blamed me for things not working out and let Bella know that. Then, five years ago, I retired from the military and took the money I had saved and bought Sunset Terrace.

The apartment complex gives me something to do and a source of income, but I'm not going to lie. Ever since I left the military, I've been floundering. There's a reason that they say it's hard to transition back to civilian life. I'm still struggling.

In a way, I know I've stopped living. I should put myself out there more and try to have a normal life like everyone else, but I can't. Not everything during my career as a Night Stalker pilot ended in sunshine and flowers. Bad things happened, things I blame myself for and can't fully get over. Good men were lost on missions and, though it wasn't directly my fault, it's a hard pill to swallow.

Guilt has a way of holding you back, not allowing you to move forward, and the faces of the men who I dropped off on a mission, but then never picked back up because they didn't make, haunt me. The only way I know how to drown the guilt is to hide away and isolate myself from the world where I can suffer in silence. Locked up in the confines of my apartment, I can drink a few beers and rehash everything. It's a bit like self-mutilation, I suppose, but the idea that good men died serving their country and protecting the ones they love bothers me.

I always thought I was a pretty mentally-tough person, but I'm not fucking Superman. There are times when I wish I had someone in my life that I could talk to, a soft feminine body that I could sink into and a future that might actually mean something.

*Dammit.* I hate when the darkness sucks me down, but sometimes it's inevitable. A shiver runs through me and I step away from the air conditioner and head into the kitchen. I open the fridge and grab a beer. As I twist the cap off, I know it's going to be one of those nights. Long and lonely. Best to start drinking now, I think, and take a long swig.

Luckily, the building keeps me pretty busy. There's always something to fix and I spend most of my time puttering around the complex with my toolbox. Most of the tenants are in their 20s, out here in search of a dream, and I look forward to catching up with them on Sundays. That's when I pull the grill out, throw some burgers and hotdogs on it and listen to them talk about their lives.

Since I don't have a life of my own, it's nice to hear about theirs. Sometimes, they even ask me for advice. I like playing the father-figure role since I don't have much opportunity to do it with my own daughter.

Hell, who am I kidding? Bella has never once asked me for advice or help in her life. To her, I'm just this guy, practically a stranger, who reaches out every once in a while and tries to force a relationship with her. Sometimes, I feel like a gnat, small, powerless and annoying, bracing myself for her inevitable swat.

I glance down at the kitchen table where a folder sits with the new tenant's paperwork. *Hailey Lane.* I hope she swings by soon because I plan on getting stinking drunk tonight. Maybe I should reach out to one of my military buddies. I haven't talked to Ryker Flynn in awhile. Last I heard, the Navy SEAL had worked through his oppressive PTSD, fallen in love, gotten married and had a baby.

I'm really glad Ryker overcame his demons and found a way to live again. Shit, he was worse off than me after losing his whole team in a Columbian jungle. Thank Christ, I wasn't involved in that clusterfuck of a mission. Last thing I need is another weight on my shoulders.

I'll text him in a day or two, I think, and drop down on the couch. Right now, I want to forget about anything military-related. I just want to sink into my couch, drink until I'm numb and forget about life. When my phone beeps, I reach over and grab it.

I sit up straight when I see Bella's name. Normally, she takes a day or two to respond so I'm surprised and happy as I open her message: *Thanks. I'm busy for the next few days, but I'll let you know.*

My heart sinks. God, I fucked up with Bella. When I should've been here, helping to raise her, I was off flying secret missions all over the world. I don't regret my time as a Night Stalker, but maybe I should've retired earlier. Maybe I should've tried harder to make things work with Paige.

Maybe, maybe, maybe.

Hindsight is always 20/20. The fact is I'm a lonely, divorced man with an estranged daughter. I have no real relationships in my life and can't even remember the last time I had sex. I rub my knuckles on my chin, feeling the light growth of scruff coming in, and think hard.

*Fuck.* Seriously, when was the last time I took a woman to bed? Last year?

I think the bigger issue is why don't I care as much as I should.

With a sigh, I finish the beer then go and grab another one. Maybe I should try online dating. I've considered it before, but then always end up rejecting the idea. I'm not very computer savvy and I think I'm far too old-fashioned to meet a woman that way.

Call me crazy, but I want to see her in person. I want to feel that spike of heat when our eyes meet for the first time. I want to hear her voice and smell her perfume. Maybe touch her hand or arm and feel the silkiness of her skin. See if there's electricity between us. You can't do any of that online. And, you'll probably have a couple of pictures that are so photoshopped that they barely resemble the real woman.

Maybe if I actually left Sunset Terrace every once in a while, I'd have the opportunity to meet a woman. *Yeah, right.* I swallow down a long drink and prop a hip against the kitchen counter. My gaze wanders out the window and zeroes in on the new girl moving into Savannah's old apartment.

Hailey Lane walks down the sidewalk to a beat-up looking pickup truck. She opens the creaky passenger door and leans inside, stretching across the seat, obviously reaching for something. She wears a tank top and tiny denim shorts, and I can't help but appreciate the way they accent her slim legs and curves. As she's rummaging around, her ass lifts higher, and I feel something I haven't felt in a long time.

A wave of desire.

I watch her pull back out and stand outside the truck for a moment. She pulls her rich chestnut hair with caramel highlights up into a messy bun and then grabs a notebook off the car's seat. After she shuts and locks the door, she heads back up the walkway and I can't look away.

*Oh, Christ, I'm turning into the creepy, old, lonely man who watches the young girls.*

When she glances over, our eyes meet for a second before I spin around. I do not want her to peg me as the building pervert. I take another swig of beer, push away from the counter and head back to the couch.

It's going to be a long night of doing nothing again.

But, back on the couch, my thoughts return to Hailey. I remember the way the sunlight highlighted her big, brown eyes. So wide and full of innocence, ready to start her life and a new adventure here in California.

She said she was from the Midwest and I wonder where exactly? And, she mentioned being a singer. I wonder if she's any good?

I don't know why I care about any of this. For Christ's sake, the girl is probably 20. Actually, I can find out exactly how old she is, I think, and stand up. I head over to her folder laying on the table and flip it open. My fingers lift her application and I scan through it.

*Hailey Lane. Twenty-three years old.*

Something in my gut tightens and not necessarily in a good way. She's a little older than I guessed, but for fuck's sake that's Bella's age. *What is wrong with me?* Enough. I shut the folder and stomp back over to the window. I spot Hailey talking to Jasmine, her next door neighbor.

Jasmine Torres is a good tenant and a little older than the other girls which makes her the mother hen of the group. She's always giving everyone advice and seems to have her life together. Wish I could say the same for myself.

The girls talk for another minute and then part ways. A part of me envies how easily these kids make friends. I don't ever remember it ever being that easy. I guess because I was always a little different than everyone else. My parents had me when they were much older. They had tried to get pregnant for years and when they finally gave up, boom! At 46, my Mom was pregnant with me.

I was their only child, a miracle baby, and grew up surrounded by their influences instead of any siblings. I learned to be polite, kind and a gentleman. I developed an affinity for vintage jazz and used to sit on the front porch with my Dad every evening after dinner and listen to it while greeting neighbors who walked by on their walks. Then, I'd watch reruns of Three's Company and Golden Girls with my Mom before bedtime. My summers were spent fishing with my Dad on a nearby lake.

Growing up in Ohio was laidback, quaint and not overly exciting, but my parents were the best and my upbringing was perfect. I never wanted for anything and they were my best friends. The sad part is, since they had me so late in life, they both passed away by the time I was 30.

I miss them. But, once they were gone, there wasn't any reason to return to Ohio. Paige and Bella were here in California. So, here I am. Trying to have a relationship with my daughter, maintain the building and start living again.

I guess I'm keeping the building up pretty well. As for the rest, I'm sucking pretty badly.

# Chapter Three: Hailey

After moving in all morning, I'm hot and exhausted. I still have to go over and sign that paperwork at Ryan's, but not before I freshen up a bit. I re-do my messy bun, check my makeup and slide some gloss over my lips. Then, I reach for my vanilla-scented perfume and spritz it all over.

Much better, I think, and head out.

I want to find out a bit more about Foxy Flyboy and when I set my mind on accomplishing something, there's no stopping me. I have a very persistent, tenacious personality so once I have a goal, I will go after something until it's mine.

And, right now, I'm determined to see if Ryan Fox could potentially be the one.

The sun is starting to lower and it's early evening as I walk past the crystal blue pool and small barbecue area. The setup here is really nice and there's a shaded area and a couple of benches. Right now, the place seems deserted. I guess everyone is at work or out pursuing a dream. Which reminds me that I need to hit the pavement and start trying to book some singing gigs as soon as possible.

At the very end of the building, I stop in front of number 7, the corner unit, and knock. A moment later, the door swings open and Ryan stands there, shirtless and only wearing a pair of worn jeans that hang low on his slim hips.

*Um, yum.* My gaze slides down his ripped chest and then pauses on his carved abs that have obviously seen thousands of crunches. There's a tattoo on his left bicep and I try not to stare too hard.

"Hey, Hailey," he says and motions for me to come in. "Thanks for coming by. I know how busy you are, trying to get settled and all." He scoops a t-shirt up, guides me over to the kitchen table and opens a folder. It's almost a crime against women when he pulls the t-shirt on and covers all those rugged muscles. "I highlighted all the places where you need to sign. It's pretty straightforward-- a one-year lease, no pets, my responsibilities and yours-- but, take your time and read through it. If you have any questions, just ask."

When he pulls a chair out for me, I sit down. "Thanks," I say and look up into those light, very intense green eyes of his. He holds a pen out and, when I take it, our fingers brush. It's like a warm current passes between us and his eyes seem to darken a shade.

*Oh, wow.* My heart skips in my chest and I force myself to look down at the paperwork, but everything is a blur. No one has ever had this kind of effect on me and it's a strange, yet exhilarating feeling. Ryan turns and I watch him head over to the fridge. He pulls out a beer and a bottle of water then offers me the water.

"Since you don't have any yet," he says and gives me the smallest wisp of a smile. "It's too hot and you've been moving all day."

I take the water from him and purposely make sure our fingers touch again. Call it an experiment. And, yep, damn, when they come into contact, I feel a zing shoot straight up my arm. "Thank you," I murmur and twist the cap off. I take a couple of gulps and try to get my head clear.

Something about Ryan Fox leaves me feeling a little unbalanced.

Maybe because I'm not used to men being kind and polite. No man has ever pulled a chair out for me before or given me ice-cold water because I'd been working all day. Usually, I'm used to getting yelled at and slapped around a little because I'm too slow or too mouthy or too something. My Uncle Wayne had no patience for me and I think he enjoyed making me feel bad about myself.

I sneak a glance up and watch Ryan crack the beer open and then take a long drink. I notice the way his throat moves when he swallows and the scruff coming in on his lower face and I feel a tug in my lower belly. Everything about him is incredibly attractive and so very masculine.

My thoughts whirl as I sign the first page. I have no idea what I'm signing and don't even care. Ryan Fox could be the Devil and I could be signing my soul over to him and I'd have no idea because I'm feeling too flustered right now to read the contract. I flip the page and sign my name on the next highlighted line.

I really want to get to know him more, but I have no idea what to say. He's so much older than me and it's a little intimidating. It's probably ridiculous to think that he'd have any interest in me. He probably likes more sophisticated women closer to his age. Nevertheless, I've never been one to back down from a challenge and I'm going to try.

I lower the pen and meet his green gaze. "I'm so glad you had a vacancy. I really love the building."

He leans a hip against the counter. "You have excellent timing because Savannah just moved out."

"Guess it was meant to be," I say and give him a smile. His eyes narrow just the slightest bit then he looks away and takes another drink. I take a good look around me and notice his place is very clean. No dirty dishes on the counter or in the sink. No crumbs anywhere. The garbage can looks nearly empty. "Your place is set up a little differently than mine. Is it bigger?"

He nods. "Yeah. Since it's on the corner, it's a little more spacious." He taps a finger on the counter and looks down at the paperwork I'm not signing.

"I'm sorry," I say and flip to the next page. "I hope I'm not keeping you."

"No, it's fine. Like I said, read through everything."

I sign my name then look up at him with a flirty smile. "Do you have any plans tonight? A big date? Or, is your girlfriend coming over?"

A muscle flexes in his jaw. "No. No big plans."

He's avoiding the rest of my questions and, after what Jasmine said, I'm pretty sure he doesn't have a girlfriend. And, I'm glad. "Yeah, me neither. Just going to unpack all weekend and get settled."

He turns to face me, leans his rear against the counter and crosses his arms. "Do you know anyone out here? Have any friends from back home here?"

I shake my head. "No. I've never even been to California until now." I see something shift in his gaze.

"If you need help with anything-- moving furniture or whatever-- don't hesitate to ask. I'm always around."

I love how polite he is and I nod. "Good to know." I take another drink of the water and decide how to let my interest in him be known. Because, yeah, I want this man to be the one. I have a feeling that Ryan Fox is exactly what I need-- a man who would be gentle, slow and get the job done without hurting me.

I let out a little sigh, remembering how good he looked with his shirt off.

"Everything okay?" he asks.

My gaze snaps up and I nod. "Actually, everything is better than it's been in a very long time." That's the truth and being here and far away from Indiana and my uncle, I feel safer. I lift up the bottled water, wrap my lips around it and drink. I've never tried to seduce a man in my life, but I watch movies and read books.

Ryan watches me, eyes glued to what I'm doing, so it seems to be working. I notice him swallow hard then push away from the counter. He turns around and looks out the window. "So, you, ah, meet any of your new neighbors yet?" he asks.

I shift in my seat and mentally will him to turn back around. I need him to look at me, to notice me, to want me. It's as though he hears me, because he slowly turns again. "I met the girl who lives next door to me, Jasmine." I cross my legs, glad that I'm wearing my shortest shorts. His green gaze dips and I feel a surge of triumph.

Ryan clears his throat. "Yeah, Jasmine is a nice girl."

*Girl.* He must think of everyone here as a girl or kid, but I need him to start viewing me as a woman. "She mentioned you used to be in the military?"

He runs a hand through his brown hair. It's a little longer than it probably should be and looks overdue for a cut. But, I really like it and wonder what it would feel like to run my fingers through it. It looks soft and thick. "That's right."

I quirk a brow, waiting for him to tell me more, but he clams up. "What branch?" I ask.

"Army. Then, I became a Night Stalker."

I frown. "What's that?"

"Part of the 160th. I was a pilot and flew special ops in and out of missions."

I get a feeling that he's being extremely modest. "Night Stalker. Sounds like a superhero."

He chuckles. "No. Just a pilot."

*Foxy Flyboy*. I wonder what he would think if he knew his nickname? I think it would be a quick way to embarrass him. "But, a pilot who must be really good."

He shrugs. "I got the job done."

"Do you still fly?"

"I haven't flown in a long time."

"But, you enjoy it?"

"I did...I do."

"So, why don't you fly anymore?"

"Do you always ask this many questions?"

My cheeks flush, but I don't break eye contact. "Maybe you could take me out flying sometime."

For a moment he doesn't say anything, but I can see the surprise flit across his face. He lets out a breath. "I told you, I don't do it anymore."

I sign the last page, stand up and summon my most flirtatious smile. "That's a shame, Ryan Fox. I would love to soar above the clouds in a tiny little plane with you."

His mouth actually drops open and it's kind of adorable.

"Thanks for the water," I say and head toward the front door, making sure to add an extra swivel in my hips just for him.

He follows me at a safe distance. I can tell he's interested, but wary. Very wary.

"I'll, ah, make a copy of the contract for you." He skirts around me and opens the door.

*So polite. Something I could definitely get used to.* "Sounds good. I'm sure I'll be seeing you around," I add with another little smile. I can feel his gaze on me as I walk back to my apartment and I'm glad.

I don't think I could have made my interest any more apparent. I've never been so brazen or forward with a man, but desperate times call for desperate measures. And, I am positively determined to make Ryan Fox my Mr. Right.

My mind is made up so now I just need for him to accept it. Hopefully, if I keep the pressure up, he will come around sooner than later. I mean, I'm not completely unfortunate looking or anything.

Back in my apartment, I know I should start setting the place up and getting unpacked, but, instead, I open my laptop, curl up in a chair and begin to make a list of potential bars and clubs where I can try to sing. And, one of them is right up the street. *No time like the present*, I think, and decide to go check it out.

Half an hour later, I walk into a hole in the wall club and sit at a table near the stage. A waitress who looks around my age comes over to take my order and, though I don't want to waste any money on a drink, I order a vodka sour.

When she returns, I say thank you and then start to ask her how I can book a gig.

"You're a singer?" she asks.

I nod. "Just moved here."

"From where?"

"Indiana."

"Oh, nice. I have family from the Midwest."

"I'm happy to finally be here, though," I say.

I'm not sure if she senses that I'm all alone or it's just a slow night and she wants to kill some time and talk, but she taps her pencil against her little notebook and leans closer. "I shouldn't say this, but this isn't the best place to sing and the owner is weird about it, anyway. If I were you, I'd go over to the Magnolia Club. Way classier and agents hang out there all the time."

"Really?" That grabs my attention. The whole point of performing is to find an agent who will help me get a record deal. "I'll definitely check it out, thank you."

"No problem. Good luck."

"I appreciate your help. I'm Hailey, by the way."

"Isa," she says. "Welcome to LaLa Land, Hailey." As a new group settles down at a nearby table, she gives me a wave and moves off.

Suddenly, I'm very happy. Tomorrow night, I'm going to head over to the Magnolia Club and check it out. In the meantime, though, I finish my drink and listen to a few performers on the small stage nearby. Not to be a jerk, but they aren't very good. I hope all of my competition is of similar caliber, but I know that won't be the case.

This city attracts the best and I need to be prepared to prove to everyone that I have what it takes to make it. And, I won't stop until I do.

On my way out, I thank Isa for her advice about the Magnolia Club. We end up talking for like 15 minutes and totally hit it off. She's really sweet and we exchange phone numbers and promise to hang out soon.

As I walk out, I can't help but smile. It feels really good to have a new friend. Actually, the second friend I've made if you count my new neighbor Jasmine.

I am definitely on a roll.

# Chapter Four: Ryan

The next day, I sit on a stool at the counter between the kitchen and living room and type on my laptop while my favorite vintage jazz plays. In one column, I write up all of the reasons why I should stay the hell away from Hailey Lane. And, there are a lot of them.

I sit back and re-read through them for the twentieth time: *she's too young; she's a tenant; she's impressionable; she doesn't know what she really wants; she's lonely because she just moved here; I'm an emotional mess and in no place to have a serious relationship; I need to focus on improving things with Bella; Bella would never approve if I dated a girl her age.*

In the opposing column, I type up one sentence: *She makes me feel things that I thought died a long time ago.*

It's so true. For whatever reason, my love life has been non-existent since I left the Night Stalkers. *Shit, who am I kidding?* It was also non-existent when I was flying secret missions all over the world. In all honesty, since my divorce from Paige, I've avoided anything serious. Getting divorced made me take a step back and acknowledge all of my faults and where things went wrong. And, I wasn't in any hurry to possibly repeat those same mistakes with someone else.

The last thing I wanted was another failed relationship. No thanks.

But, it's also a very lonely way to live and I think it's finally taking its toll on me. I used to just ignore it and pretend everything was fine. But, it was a lot easier to do that when I was busy. Now I have too much time on my hands to think. And, lately, I've missed having a woman's warm body on my arm and in my bed. Not just any woman, though. I yearn for that spark with someone special.

And, I fucking felt it with Hailey.

I read through all of the reasons why she's off-limits again and then add one more: *I'm old enough to be her dad.*

Despite that and everything else I wrote, she's such a temptation. The girl is dangerous and I have to stay away from her. My gaze wanders over to the positive column and I type out another sentence: *She makes me want to live again.*

I feel sad. It's like there's something potentially really good in front of me, but I need to just ignore it and be a goddamn martyr because that is what's best for everyone. For Hailey, for Bella...well, not for me, but that's where the sacrifice comes in.

*Oh, for fuck's sake.* There are plenty of fish in the sea, I tell myself, and pull up a dating website. At this point, I'm just going to join. What's the worst thing that could happen? No one will message me? So, what? I can message them myself.

Even though I hate this dating online bullshit, I start to fill out the application. It's stupid, shallow and doesn't tell you anything that's actually important about a person you could potentially have a relationship with, but I force myself to do it.

*What's your story?* I write that I'm a divorced father looking to meet someone special when I should write that I'm tired of being lonely and need to have sex with a woman. Preferably soon.

*What do you do for a living?* Own and manage an apartment complex. The truth is more along the lines of re-live my failures and drown my sorrows and loneliness in alcohol.

*Are you a cat or dog person?* I type in dog because I do like them, but there's a no-pet policy here so the question is moot.

*What's your star sign?* Virgo. Which means I am a perfectionist, picky and it's hard to get my attention. Unless, of course, you're Hailey Lane.

*Are you close to your family?* What family? My daughter rarely speaks to me and my parents are long-gone. But, I write a simple yes so I don't sound like a complete psycho.

*If you could be a character in any movie, who would you be?* God, these are the stupid, fucking questions I hate. I get it, you're supposed to come up with something witty, but I'm not feeling particularly inspired right now so I just write Maverick in Top Gun. At least then I can fly.

There's a knock on the door and I glance up. I'm not expecting anyone, but that's usually the case. Probably a tenant, I think, and walk over and open the door.

Hailey stands there looking edible in a tight, little t-shirt and tiny denim shorts again. *God, she's going to kill me.* "Hailey, what can I do for you?" When I realize I'm clenching my fists, I loosen them and force what I hope looks like a smile.

"Hi, Ryan. I hope I'm not bothering you, but I kind of need a man's help."

"Uh, sure." Since I offered to help her earlier, I have to keep my promise.

"Great!" Her big brown eyes light up. "Got a hammer?"

"Yeah." My toolbox lays nearby and I grab it.

Hailey motions for me to follow her. "I have a couple of pictures I want to hang up."

We walk over to her place and it looks like she's unpacked a few boxes, but she still has a lot to do. Hailey grabs a picture of Billie Holiday and walks over to a wall where she holds it up. "What do you think?" she asks and wiggles her ass.

*Christ.* I instantly go hard and feel my nostrils flare. As my very lonely cock makes its presence known, I swing the toolbox in front of my zipper and pull my gaze up to the picture. "You like jazz?" I ask.

"Billie, Ella and Etta were incomparable. I love to sing their songs. No one even comes close and the stuff on the radio today....It's garbage."

I just blink. That's exactly how I feel.

"I don't know. I guess I'm an old soul," she says.

*Yeah, me, too.* Even so, she's still too young. *Bella's age, Ryan, I remind myself. Don't forget that.*

When I feel like I'm back under control, I set the toolbox down and pull the hammer out and a nail out. I walk over and grasp the edge of the frame. "Go back there and tell me how it looks," I say, the nail between my teeth.

With a nod, Hailey moves back and cocks her head. "A little higher," she says. "And, a bit to the left."

Sexual thoughts fill my head and I swallow hard. I wonder how she likes it. *No, no you don't.* But, yes, yes, I do.

*Fuck.*

"Okay, perfect. That's the spot."

My eyes slide shut. *For the love of God.* I lower the picture and pound the nail in with more force than I intend. I'm lucky the plaster doesn't crack. Then, I hang up the picture of Billie with her ever-present gardenia tucked behind an ear. "How's it look?"

"Very good job. Thank you. I'm terrible at hanging pictures up and it would've turned out all crooked. Then, I'd re-do it ten times and there'd be a bunch of holes in the wall."

"I'm glad I came over to help you," I say in a dry voice and she laughs. It's a low, sultry sound and I like it.

"And, I'm sure you wouldn't have liked it when I filled all the holes with toothpaste."

I cringe. "You're one of those people, huh?"

She smiles.

"That's a pet peeve of mine," I tell her. "I'm a firm believer in spackle."

"What else are you a firm believer in?" she asks and takes a step closer.

Call me crazy, but she emphasized the word firm. There's no way she could've known. I had the damn toolbox in front of me. But, I can't help but wonder. "I'm not sure I know what you mean," I say.

"Ryan…"

Her big, brown eyes dip and she's checking me out, I realize. It should make me uncomfortable, but it doesn't. Quite the opposite, actually. Those dark eyes running over me are turning me on. "I should probably go," I say.

"Do you like me?" she asks out of the blue.

"What?" I hiss.

She walks right up to me. "Because I really like you," she says and looks up at me.

For being so bold, she also looks extremely shy. Like she can't believe the words are coming out her mouth. Hell, neither can I.

"I'm never this forward," she admits.

"Of course, I…like you," I manage.

"I don't mean as a friend." She reaches out and touches my arm. I know I should pull away, but I don't. I glance down and watch as she runs those delicate fingers up and down my bicep. It makes my cock surge to life again, but this time I don't turn away or try to hide it.

"Hailey, it's been a while so my self-control isn't very strong right now," I warn her.

When she looks up at me, she looks like a beautiful temptress and I start to feel my restraint crumble.

"It's been 23 years for me," she says.

"Christ," I swear. She's telling me she's a virgin. But, why?

"But, I'd like to change that. With somebody like you."

*Oh. That's why.*

"I have to go," I say and jerk away from her. I grab my toolbox and practically trip my way over to the front door. Before I leave, I turn, give her my most serious and somber expression and use my best Dad voice. "It's not going to happen between us, Hailey. I'm sorry, but the answer is no."

As I close the door behind me, I'm so hot and bothered that it's ridiculous. I have a feeling I could've just banged that little girl's brains out and a part of me is disgusted with myself because I wanted to. I run a frustrated hand through my hair and stomp back over to my apartment.

I need to do something about this raging hard-on, I think. It's been a while, but I grab my phone and search through my contacts for Jessica's number. She's my old "friend with benefits" and I start writing a text out to her. God, my fingers are shaking. It's such an obvious booty call, but that's all we ever were to each other.

I hit send and drop down on the couch. *C'mon, Jess, I need you tonight. I need you badly.*

I stare at my phone screen, willing it to light up with a response. Fucking nothing. I'm getting so aggravated that I don't know what to do with myself. Maybe she found some other guy to call when the need arose.

I don't think I've ever been this sexually frustrated before. It's like the past couple of years just hit me with the force of a freight train and I need it now. Need it badly. That little tease in apartment 12 is going to be my undoing.

When my phone beeps, I swipe it up and read Jessica's response: *Hey, handsome. Haven't heard from you in awhile. FYI, I got married about a year and a half ago. Hope you're well.*

A year and a half ago? Holy hell, it's been longer than I thought since I got laid. No wonder I'm going crazy. Without any other option, I unzip my pants and just take care of things myself. Afterwards, I feel better, but not satisfied.

I wander back over to my laptop, sit down and finish the stupid dating profile. When it comes time to upload a picture, I settle on one I have from my days as a Night Stalker. Dark hair short, sunglasses on, helmet tucked under an arm, I'm in uniform and stand beside an Apache helicopter. It's a pretty badass shot and makes me look important. Back when I was doing important things.

*There, all done.* Hopefully, some woman out there in cyberland takes an interest in me and my ass will go out on a date and get laid. At this point, that's all I want. Forget love and a relationship. I have to remember to not be overly selective or come off as too needy. I need to remember that and-

I tilt my head and hear something. It sounds like...singing. I stand up and walk over to the open window and frown. A light breeze blows in and it seems to also usher in the prettiest voice I've ever heard.

I immediately know that it's Hailey and she has the voice of an angel.

And, then I realize she's singing an old Billie Holiday song called Lover Man. Of course, she is. Anything to torture me. I press my head against the window pane as the lyrics flow over me. "I don't know why, but I'm feeling so sad. I long to try something I never had. Never had no kissing. Oh, what I've been missing. Lover man, oh, where can you be?"

My eyes slide shut and I picture Hailey singing. Naked.

"The night is cold and I'm so alone. I'd give my soul just to call you my own. Got a moon above me. But no one to love me. Lover man, oh, where can you be?"

She calls to me like a siren and I know all I have to do is walk back over there and she'd fall into my arms.

"I've heard it said," she sings, "That the thrill of romance can be like a heavenly dream. I go to bed with a prayer that you'll make love to me. Strange as it seems. Someday we'll meet and you'll dry all my tears. Then whisper sweet, little things in my ear. Hugging and a-kissing. Oh, what we've been missing. Lover man, oh, where can you be?"

*I'm here, Hailey,* I think.

Then, I shut the window and go take a cold shower.

# Chapter Five: Hailey

The next day, I'm unpacking and wondering where I went wrong with Ryan. I messed up big-time and he ran out of here so fast, my head spun. Maybe I came on too strong? But, time is of the essence. If my Uncle Wayne shows up here…

I shiver even though it's almost 90 degrees outside already.

As I'm organizing my coffee table books, there's a knock on the door. I imagine it can only be Jasmine or Ryan since I don't know anyone else here yet. I hope it's Ryan and he's ready to jump my bones. I open the door and two guys around my age stand there.

"Hey, neighbor," the taller one says. "I'm Cody and this is Mason." He nods to his buddy who stands beside him. "We live upstairs and wanted to welcome you to the complex."

"Hi," Mason says. He seems the shyer one of the two and they both are extremely tan with sun-streaked hair. Typical California boys.

"Hi, I'm Hailey," I say and they shake my hand.

"So, how's it going? Need any help with anything?" Cody asks and glances over my shoulder at the mess that I'm still trying to organize.

*Yeah, if I need help, I'll go to Ryan.* "I'm good," I say. "But, thanks."

Just then, a very pretty girl with her dark red hair pulled back into a tight, low bun walks by. "Is the Dynamic Duo bothering you already?" she asks.

The boys just shake their head and the redhead hits Cody in the shoulder. "Stop harassing my new neighbor." She turns to me and smiles. "I'm Taylor and live right there." She points to the apartment on the opposite side of Jasmine's place. She wears a leotard and a cute sheer pink skirt.

"I'm Hailey. Are you a ballerina?" I ask.

"Ballerina-in-the-making," she says. "I take classes during the day and then dance at a nearby club at night. Gotta pay the bills til I make it as a prima ballerina."

"That's really cool. It takes a lot of work to do classical ballet."

"Tell me about it." She laughs.

"C'mon," Cody teases. "She does a couple of fancy spins. No big deal."

Taylor props a hand on her hip. "Says the bum who goes out on a surfboard and catches a few waves. I mean, how hard could that be?'

"Why don't you come out some time and I'll show you?"

"It's not as easy as it looks," Mason adds.

"Same with ballet, boys," Taylor says.

"Ah, we're just busting your balls," Cody says. "But, if you two ever want a surfing lesson, let us know."

I look at Taylor and she rolls her eyes. "I'd be scared of sharks," I say.

The guys chuckle. "They don't bother anybody," Cody says.

"Well, usually they don't," Mason adds.

"We're going to play pool tonight. You ladies wanna come?" Cody asks.

Taylor looks at me and lifts a brow. "I could play. You wanna come, Hailey?"

"Sure," I say. I'm excited to make some more new friends and, after Ryan's rejection, I could use some fun.

"Let me take a shower and change first," Taylor says.

Mason looks down at his watch. "Cool. Why don't we go over in an hour?"

"Sounds good," Taylor says. "Hailey, come over to my place when you're ready."

I nod and wave goodbye. I spend the next half hour freshening up and then I head over to Taylor's. My gaze is on Ryan's place when she pulls the door open. "Hey, c'mon in."

I look around and her place is decorated with all kinds of dancing things. Framed posters of famous ballerinas and really cool pictures of people dancing. I walk closer and study one of the images of a couple locked in a heated embrace. It looks like they're doing the tango and Taylor walks up beside me. "I love Fabian Perez. His artwork is just amazing. So full of passion and fire. Makes me almost want a man in my life."

"Right?" I say, thinking of Ryan and what it would be like to be caught up in his embrace.

"So, what's up with you? Did you leave your boyfriend back home?"

"Me?" I laugh. "No."

"What's so funny?"

I shake my head. "There wasn't a very big selection of eligible men in Indiana. And, I don't think the man I'm interested in is all that into me," I admit.

Her blue eyes go wide. "You like someone here?"

*Oops.* I probably shouldn't have said anything.

"C'mon, spill it."

"No, there's nobody."

She eyes me then, thankfully, drops it when Mason and Cody show up. The four of us walk down to a neighborhood bar that's pretty quiet. We order a round of beers and gather around one of the pool tables.

"You a pool shark, Indiana?" Mason asks and bumps me with his elbow.

"How did you know I was from Indiana?" I ask.

"Word gets around pretty fast at Sunset Terrace."

I look up into his blue eyes and, for a moment, consider him as a solution to my current cirmcumstance. He's young, nice and definitely cute. I don't think it would be too hard to get him to hook up with me. But, then I picture Ryan's green eyes and know that's who I really want.

I just need to figure out a way to convince him.

"So, why did you move to L.A.?" Cody asks and racks the balls.

"To be a singer."

"Very cool. I think you're the only singer in the building. It's mostly a bunch of actors."

"Is that what you guys want to do?"

"Oh, hell no," Cody says.

"We're pro-surfers," Mason adds.

"Oh! I didn't realize you were professionals. You must get to travel all over, huh?"

"Sure do. We leave next week for a competition in Hawaii."

"So, if you want that surf lesson," Mason says with a wink, "it'll have to be when we get back."

"She's scared of sharks, dummy," Taylor says and lifts her pool stick. She takes aim and breaks the balls apart. They roll everywhere and Mason steps up to go next. He shoots a ball straight into the side pocket.

"Watch out," Cody warns. "My buddy here is pretty good."

"Damn straight," he says and takes another turn, sinking another ball.

Taylor leans a hip against the table. "This may take awhile," she says. "So, what do you think of Cali and Sunset Terrace so far?"

"I love it," I say, my voice full of enthusiasm.

"I'm so glad you moved into Savannah's old place and not some boring old accountant or something."

"Jasmine said Savannah moved in with her boyfriend?"

Taylor gives a little sigh. "Nick Knight. He's dreamy."

"Isn't he like 40-something?" Cody asks.

"Really?" I ask. "And, how old is Savannah?"

"Savvy is our age. So, yeah, they've got the older man/younger woman thing going on and it's hot." Taylor fans herself.

"Your turn," Mason tells me.

I step up and hit the ball, but it really doesn't go anywhere because I'm too busy thinking about what Taylor just said. "And, it's not weird?" I ask.

"What do you mean?" Taylor chalks the end of her stick.

"The age difference?"

"No. They're adorable together and so in love. It's kinda sickening," she adds with a grin.

*Hmm.* Then, maybe I'm not completely crazy to think I can catch Ryan's interest.

"Babe, go get us another round," Cody says and taps Taylor's bum with his stick.

"Get it yourself, *babe.*" She rolls her eyes. I've noticed that Taylor is the epitome of a feisty redhead with lots of sass and fire.

"I'll get it," I offer and head over to the bar. I place the order and lean forward, glancing at all the bottles on the shelves. I'm not a big drinker, but I do like a beer or girly drink when I'm out with friends. All that hard liquor, though, would probably make me sick.

"Hi."

I look over my shoulder and see a cute guy who looks around 25 with dirty blond hair. "Hi," I say.

"One of those guys your boyfriend?" he asks and nods to Mason and Cody.

I shake my head and he gives me a bright, white smile. "So, it's okay if I talk to you?"

"Sure."

"I'm Alex."

"Nice to meet you. I'm Hailey."

I end up talking to Alex for another 10 minutes. He's funny in a sarcastic sort of way and definitely friendly enough the way he keeps touching my arm. I glance down at the sweating beers on the bar and nod to the pool table. "I should get back to my friends," I say.

"Sure," he says and I start to gather the beers up. "Any chance you aren't busy tomorrow night?" he asks.

"Maybe," I say with a little smile.

"Well, maybe I'd like to take you out."

*Wow, guys here are pretty forward*, I think. "Um, sure."

"Cool." He pulls out his phone and asks for my number. A minute later, I head back over to the pool table and hand everyone a beer.

"Did you just give that guy your number?" Taylor asks.

I smile. "Yeah."

We both burst into giggles. "He's really cute."

"Uh, excuse me," Cody says. "But, what about us? We are way better looking than that dude."

Taylor punches his arm. "But, we love you like a brother."

"Speak for yourself, Tay, and let Hailey decide who she has the hots for."

I know exactly who I have the hots for, but I can't tell them. Instead, I just smile and sip my beer.

My date with Alex is here before I know it. I spend some extra time getting ready and wear a cute, little sundress and sandals. I let my long brown hair hang loose even though it's warm out and spray myself with my favorite vanilla perfume.

I can't say that I have high hopes or anything, but if Ryan isn't interested in me then I'm going to have to pursue other avenues.

Alex takes me out to a hip sushi place here in Hollywood and I feel bad, but I don't like seafood. *At all.* Just the smell makes me nauseous and when we walk into the restaurant, my stomach turns.

I end up eating some ramen noodles and white rice while he orders a lot of smelly, fishy things. *Ugh.* The thought of him kissing me goodnight makes me want to run for the hills. He seems like a nice guy, I guess, but within 20 minutes, I know he's not the one for me.

Problem is, I keep comparing him to Ryan and Alex is no Ryan Fox. Ryan is taller, better looking and such a gentleman. Alex may be more my age, but he seems a little immature. All he talks about is getting drunk and partying with celebrities. He also really likes the Dodgers because he talks about them. A lot.

I've barely said more than a few sentences all night and he hasn't asked me much of anything. But, he likes to talk about himself and I know more about Alex Petty than I could ever want to know. Especially since I decide I will not be going on a second date with him.

After dinner, he asks if I want to go get a drink, but all I want to do is go home. When I tell him I'm tired, he looks annoyed. But, why prolong the evening when I know that I'm not interested? I hate wasting people's time.

When we pull up to Sunset Terrace, Alex hops out and, to my dismay, seems intent on walking me up to my door. All I can think about is his fishy breath and I even offered him a mint earlier, but he declined.

At my door, I turn to say goodnight, hoping to make it quick, when he catches me completely by surprise and yanks me against him. I gasp right before his mouth covers mine in a rough kiss. He forces his tongue into my mouth and I push against his chest.

But, he's stronger. I try to twist away and finally manage to break my lips free. "Let me go," I say and shove. He ignores me, though, dips his head and begins kissing my neck.

"C'mon, baby. Aren't you going to invite me in?"

When I feel his hand slide up my thigh and under my skirt, I try to squirm away. "No!"

All of a sudden, Alex flies back through the air and drops to the ground. I blink in surprise when Ryan steps out of the shadows and, in a low growl, says, "She said no, asshole."

My heart thunders in my chest at the dark, ferocious look on his face. It's a little scary and I never imagined this dark side of him. I just assumed that Ryan was the nice guy, a little on the shy side and definitely not the physical type. Not this dominant, intimidating, half-feral man that looks like he's ready to beat the ever-living crap out of Alex.

But, I suddenly feel safe and I watch Alex scramble up.

"Screw you," he says.

Ryan fakes a lurch in his direction and Alex takes off, running back to his car. Then, Ryan turns those intense green eyes on me. "Are you okay?"

He looks like a wild animal and I let out a breath and press a hand to my chest. "Yeah, I think so. Thanks to you."

"Who the hell was that guy?"

"My date."

Green lightning strikes in his eyes and I know he is not happy.

# Chapter Six: Ryan

I shove a hand through my hair and glare at the car that squeals away from the curb. "Where'd you find that loser?"

Hailey shifts, looking uncomfortable. "He seemed nicer last night at the bar."

I grit my teeth together so I don't say anything rude. *The bar? Jesus Christ.* "C'mon, let's get you inside."

As Hailey unlocks the door, I feel a wave of fury pound through me when I think of how that kid had his hand shoved up under her dress. She doesn't deserve someone who is rough and forcing her to do things she obviously didn't want to fucking do. The more I think about the situation, the angrier I get.

"Hailey, this isn't Indiana. Los Angeles is full of creeps and you can't trust everyone you meet."

She shuts the door, looks up at me and narrows those normally big, brown eyes. "Trust me, I'm safer here than there. And, I appreciate your help, but I don't need a lecture."

I clench my hands and force myself to calm down. I'm pissed. Pissed at that guy for forcing himself on her and pissed at her because she's not taking this seriously. "What would you have done if I hadn't come along?" I ask. "He had his hand up your fucking skirt, Hailey, and he wasn't backing down."

I need to rein it in, calm down, but the idea of someone hurting Hailey is turning me inside out. Making me see red and I breathe hard, chest heaving, as I wait for her to answer.

"Why are you so upset?" she asks.

"I'm not!" I roar. *Fuck*. What the hell is wrong with me? I'm coming off as a damn lunatic. I pinch the bridge of my nose and squeeze my eyes shut. Why am I being so possessive? Hailey Lane isn't mine. She's free to see whoever she wants.

When I open my eyes and look at her, a sadness flashes through her chocolate eyes. "I wish you could've been in Indiana with me when things got bad. You can get scary fast."

My heart twists in my chest. "Someone hurt you?"

She nods and then drops down on the couch. I know I should leave, but I can't ignore the pull between us. I walk over and sit down beside her. "Do you want to talk about it?" Everything within me wants to make her feel better.

"My parents died in a car accident when I was 16 and I went to live with my aunt and uncle. At first, it was okay, but when my aunt died last year, things got bad."

I wait for her to continue and she clasps her hands together.

"My Uncle Wayne was always distant and kind of cold toward me. After my aunt died, he turned downright mean. He became verbally and physically abusive. I spent the last year dodging his fist and saving every dime so I could get away."

"Hailey, I'm sorry." I don't even think twice. Just reach out and squeeze her hand. Someone *hit* her? Every atom in every cell of my body yearns to return the favor to the fucker.

"Some bad things happened," she says vaguely, "and I left in the middle of the night so he wouldn't know right away. Now that I'm finally gone, I need to get rid of all the baggage from there." She swallows hard. "Including my virginity."

I realize I'm still holding her hand. "Why do you have to get rid of it?"

"I wouldn't expect you to understand, but it's just a painful reminder of-" her voice falters. "Of my life in Indiana."

I get the feeling she's leaving something out, but I know it's none of my business. Even though I'm curious as hell. I want to know because I have the urge to help. But, I'm still mad when I think about the idiot she was just with. "So, you were just going to throw it away on that punk?" I don't mean to sound harsh, but I can hear the abrasive tone in my voice.

"I don't want to throw it away," she said. "Otherwise, I'd be with him right now. I want it to be with someone experienced and gentle and kind." She hesitates and then the next sentence rushes out. "Someone like you."

I hiss in a breath.

"I don't suppose you're interested?" she asks.

She can't be serious. I finally let go of her hand and study her face. God, she's beautiful. But, so naive. "You don't even know me. Your first time should be with someone special. With a man who will take care of you."

"A man like you."

"Don't say that."

"Why not? It's true."

It is true. I would take my time and bring her so much pleasure. Just the thought of spending the night with her fills my head with all sorts of naughty ideas and my groin tightens.

"I should go." I stand up. Then, a moment of indecision flickers inside me. Why am I fighting it? I'm attracted to her, she's throwing herself at me and, God knows, I want to have sex. *No. Go, Ryan. She doesn't know what she wants. Not really.*

I walk over to the door and then make the mistake of turning around. She's following me, right behind me, and she runs a hand up my arm. I feel like I was just shocked. "The offer's on the table, Foxy Flyboy. Please, think about it."

*Foxy Flyboy?* I give her a strange look and she shrugs.

"It's what all the girls here call you."

I reach behind me, fumble with the door knob and walk out. If I don't leave now there's a good chance I won't leave at all tonight.

As I stalk back to my apartment, I can't help but think about her last comment.

Foxy Flyboy.

*That's what all the girls call me?* I had no idea and I guess I should be flattered. I just assumed they viewed me as older and more like a father figure. *Huh.*

Safely back inside my place, I go straight to the fridge and crack open a beer. It's going to be another long, lonely night. Hailey's invitation echoes through my head and it's a damn tempting offer. I massage my temple with a couple of fingers and wonder why I always have to try to do the right thing.

All my life, I've been the guy to think about everyone else's feelings and problems first. I always put my wants and needs second because I'm so worried about pleasing other people. Maybe that should stop.

For once in my life, maybe I should put myself first.

If I didn't have a daughter about Hailey's age, I don't think this would be such a dilemma for me. It's pretty clear that I want her and she wants me. But, I'm so hung up on the fact that she's only 23.

*Does it really matter, though?* I ask myself. Older men date younger women all the time and nobody thinks anything of it. If anything, those men are considered a catch.

Here's the other thing. If she's bound and determined to lose her virginity, it should be with a man who will be respectful and take care of her needs first. Not some creep who won't deserve her or even understand the amount of trust she's placing in him. Not some punk who will probably be too hard, too fast and not take the time to introduce her to something as important as sex.

When I think about it like that, it seems like the right thing to do is step up and do the deed myself.

I want to make sure she's taken care of and I would do exactly that. *Shit.* I can't believe I'm actually considering this. But, the alternative-- to let someone else use and take advantage of her-- leaves a sick feeling in the pit of my stomach.

There have to be some ground rules, though.

First of all, it could only be one night. And, I would make it a night that neither of us would ever forget.

Second, it would be a mutually-beneficial arrangement. No emotions or feelings involved. Only sex.

And, third, it couldn't be here at Sunset Terrace. We would have to go to a hotel or somewhere away from gossiping neighbors. A place where no one would see us.

I don't think she'd have any problem with my terms. The real question is can I go through with it? The more I think about it, the more I think I can.

The more I want to do it.

# Chapter Seven: Hailey

When Sunday rolls around, I find myself out by the pool with Jasmine on one side and Taylor on the other. Cody and Mason splash around in the pool and Ryan just fires the grill up. I watch him closely behind my sunglasses, but he's focused on messing around with a package of hotdog buns.

I roll my eyes and start to feel bad about myself. I practically threw myself at him last night. I basically said, "Hey, here's my virginity. It's all yours if you want it."

And, he didn't want it.

I know I'm a pretty girl and I've never had any low self-esteem issues, but Ryan's rejection is making me doubt myself. I've always been under the impression that most men like younger, innocent women.

But, Ryan Fox isn't like most men.

When he bends over and scoops a soda out of the cooler, my gaze drops to his perfect ass. Then, Jasmine squeals beside me. She jumps up and hurries down to the curb where a Mustang just rolled up.

"Savvy!" she cries and embraces a tall, thin, drop-dead gorgeous blonde. An even taller, dark-haired man walks around the car, leading a dog on a leash, and slips his hand into hers. Then, the trio starts toward us. Jasmine and Savannah chat a mile a minute.

"Is that Savannah?" I ask Taylor.

"Yep," she says and waves to them. "Isn't Nick scrumptious?"

The former model looks like he just stepped off a runway, but I can't help but look back over at Ryan. Less pretty boy and more rugged, Ryan is more my type. As they walk up, Jasmine introduces me to Nick and Savannah.

They remind me of Brad and Angelina when they first started dating. So good-looking that you can't look directly at them or you'll die from the sheer beauty. "Hi," I say. "I just moved into your old place."

"So nice to meet you," Savannah says. "Isn't Sunset Terrace great?"

"I love it," I say and laugh when the shepherd mix sniffs me with his big, wet nose.

"This is Paul," Nick says.

"Hello, Paul." I pet him and he gives me a kiss. Savannah pulls up a lounge chair, lowers herself down and places a hand over her lower stomach.

"How are you feeling?" Jasmine asks.

"Well, the morning sickness has been morning, afternoon *and* night sickness. So, I'll try not to throw up while I'm here," she promises.

"You're pregnant?" I ask and she nods. She wears a loose-fitting shirt and still looks thin to me. Probably because she's so incredibly tall and slim naturally. "Congratulations."

"They're having twins!" Taylor announces.

"Oh, wow."

"Tell me about it," Nick says and we all laugh.

After a few more questions about the babies, Savannah launches into a story about vet school while Nick and Paul wander over to talk to Ryan. They shake hands and after Nick grabs a cold drink, they sit in a couple of chairs in the shade, the dog stretched out in the grass by Nick's feet.

I look from Nick back to Savannah and their age gap is no secret. It's clear that she's in her early 20s and he's in his early 40s. Yet, it works. From what I can tell, and from the sly looks they keep exchanging, it works really well.

I really hope that Ryan notices, too. I can tell he's hung up on our age difference for some stupid reason, but Nick sure isn't bothered by that at all.

Of course, there's also the possibility that Ryan just doesn't like me. That I'm not his type.

"Hailey?"

I look back over at the girls around me. Someone just asked me something and I'm not sure who or what. "Hmm?"

"I asked if you booked any gigs yet?" Jasmine adjusts the stack of bright, fun bracelets on her wrist, but her gaze is too keen and I'm pretty sure she saw me watching Ryan.

"What kind of stuff do you sing?" Savannah asks.

"Oh, um, I like a lot of things, but especially jazz standards."

"You should try to get a gig at the Magnolia Club. Nick took me there last week and the place was packed. It would be a great place for you to sing."

"I just sent them an email with a demo song."

"You'll get it," Taylor says. "I heard you singing the other night and you are really good."

A blush creeps up over my cheeks. "Thanks."

"When did you start singing?" Savannah asks.

*After my parents died. The moment I realized I had no one left in the world who loved me. When my uncle started beating on me.* "I think I was about 16," I say. "I guess it was my way of escaping everyday life."

"I always wished I could sing," Taylor says.

"You are a fantastic dancer. You don't need to sing, too," Jasmine says.

"Yeah, leave something for the rest of us."

They laugh and it's nice to be surrounded by a group of girls, a potential circle of new friends. I didn't leave any friends behind in Indiana. I was too busy working down at the diner, taking every available shift and saving every penny so I could escape.

"We need to plan a girls' night out," Taylor says. "You guys all need to come to Club Noir when I'm working and I will hook you up with a VIP table and drinks tickets."

"I could use a night of dancing and drinking," Jasmine says and adjusts her oversized hat. "What's everyone's schedule like?"

"I have class every day, so a Friday or Saturday night works best for me," Savannah says. "I can't guarantee that I'll be able to stay out too late, though. I'm usually sound asleep by nine lately."

"I have a trip scheduled this week, but I'll be back Thursday."

"Where are you going, Jazz?"

"The Big Apple. Got a fitting for the Givenchy show coming up."

Jasmine Torres walks the most prestigious runways for top designers and she doesn't blink or brag about it. "That's exciting," I say.

"It's just work. No biggie." Jasmine bumps Savannah's elbow. "If I see your billboard, I'll send you a picture."

Savannah laughs. "Oh, gosh, I don't know if I want to see myself that big in the middle of New York City. How embarrassing."

"Savvy booked a couple huge Guess campaigns," Jasmine explains.

"And, I thank God every day," she says with a dreamy smile and glances over at Nick.

"Why don't I ever meet any hot men at my work?" Taylor asks.

"Because they're either gay ballet dancers or drunk creeps," Jazz says.

"Sad, but true," Taylor says. "Okay, so how about you, Hailey? How does Friday night sound?"

"Until I book a gig, I'm pretty free."

"Great! I'm putting you all on the VIP list and we are going to have a much-needed girls' night out on the town."

"What about Morgan?" Savannah asks. "Has anyone seen her lately?"

Jasmine shakes her head. "Poor thing. Last I heard, her Mom wasn't doing that well."

"I feel awful for her," Taylor says. "I wish there was something we could do."

I look from one girl to the next, not sure what they're talking about.

"Morgan lives over in number 2," Jazz says, "but, I'm guessing you probably haven't met her yet. She's always working. Her mom is sick and she's got hospital bills and her mom's care to pay for."

"That's so sad," I say.

Taylor nods. "She's an actor, but doesn't get to go out on many auditions because she's always taking on extra shifts at her real job."

I understand that better than anyone and feel a wave of sympathy for the girl.

"I'll invite her if I see her," Jasmine says, "but, we all know she won't come. She doesn't let herself do anything but work. I can tell that it's starting to take its toll on her, too. She always looks so tired and unhappy."

"God, that girl needs a night off more than any of us," Taylor says.

All of a sudden, Cody and Mason grab Savannah in big, wet bear hugs and she screeches. "Enough girly talk," Cody says, blocking our sun and dripping pool water all over.

"Hey, watch where you're dripping," Jazz says and he instantly shakes like a dog, spraying all of us with water droplets.

We all cry out and then Ryan announces that the food is ready. The smell of burgers and hotdogs on the grill hits my nose and my stomach growls. Everyone grabs a paper plate and bun and then Ryan flips either a burger or hotdog onto them.

I hang back, making sure I'm last in line and everyone else has wandered off and settled down to eat. When I move up beside him with my plate, he spears a hotdog and places it in the bun.

"Thanks," I say.

"You're welcome." He avoids eye contact with me, pretending that I didn't ask him to sleep with me last night.

And, it annoys me.

"Ryan?"

Finally, he looks up and those light green eyes seem to simmer. Today, they remind me of the grass in springtime and I want to sink into their depths.

"Have you thought anymore about…my offer?"

I see him suck in a breath. "Yeah, and the answer is still no."

My heart sinks. Then, I get pissed. "Fine. Guess I'll just have to find someone else." When I turn to stomp away, he grabs my arm.

"What's the damn rush? Take your time. Find someone special."

"Don't lecture me," I snap and pull my arm away. "I'm getting rid of it whether you'll help me or not." Okay, that was a bit of a threat, but maybe it would light a fire under his ass.

I walk back over to the group and sit down beside Taylor. I don't think anyone noticed what just happened between me and Ryan until I glance over and see the strange look on Taylor's face. But, she doesn't comment. Just frowns and bites into her burger.

A moment later, Ryan pulls up a chair on the outer circle of our group and sits. It's clear he doesn't feel completely comfortable and hangs in the background. And, of course, I feel bad for him even though I'm still mad at him.

*Annoying, alluring, infuriating man.*

Even though I avoid looking his way, I can feel his gaze on me. It's like when you stand too close to a roaring fire. The heat seeps into your pores and feels good at first, but then it suddenly starts to burn. When I finally look up, his piercing green eyes hold mine for a moment too long.

Then, he looks away.

I want to scream. He's sending me mixed signals, thrusting me away, and then those beautiful minty-green eyes of his tell a completely different story.

*I'm going to try one more time,* I decide. Then, if he pushes me away, I'm not going to waste another minute on Ryan Fox.

Later that night, my apartment is stuffy and I wander outside for some fresh air. It's cooler out here and I sit down on the bench beneath the trees. It's around ten o'clock and the moon is high in the sky and the sting of Ryan's rejection is like a splinter under my skin. It hurts, but thoughts of him won't go away.

I look over to the large kitchen window of his apartment and see a light on. I wonder what he's doing. The window is open, but the curtains hang still since there's no breeze tonight. Suddenly, my phone rings and I glance down at the caller id. *Unknown.* Thinking it may be a club, I answer. "Hello?"

And, I wish to God I hadn't.

My Uncle Wayne's gravelly voice comes over the line and, even though he's thousands of miles away, it still makes me shiver as though he's standing right beside me. "Hailey, girl, where the hell are you?' he demands.

"Gone," I say. "And, I'm not coming back."

"The gal down at the diner said you up and went to Cal-ee-fornia. Is that true?"

My heart plummets. *Dammit, I didn't want him finding out. What does it matter, though? It's not like he's going to come out and visit.* "It's none of your business," I tell him.

"Like hell," he rumbles across the line. "You were my meal ticket."

"No," I say, my voice rising. "It's not my job to pay off your debts."

"He agreed to the deal. You didn't have a say," my uncle thunders.

I shake my head and tears prick the backs of my eyes. "It's my body."

"You're an ungrateful little-"

I hang up. My phone rings again, but I turn the ringer off and silent tears start to stream down my face. When Ryan's door opens, I swipe the wetness away and pretend not to notice. But, he walks over and sits down beside me.

"Are you okay? You sounded upset."

*Great*. So, the whole complex probably heard me yell at my uncle. I want to tell him yes, that I'm fine, but something inside me finally breaks. "No," I whisper, unable to look at him. Instead, I focus on my painted toenails and struggle not to cry. But, to my utter humiliation, the tears begin to roll down my cheeks and hit the grass.

Ryan heaves out a breath, reaches over and tilts my chin up. "Hey, it's alright." He wipes a tear away and I burst like a dam. "Hailey…"

The next thing I know, I'm in Ryan's arms and sobbing my heart out. I've held my emotions back for too long and now they pour out of me and there's nothing I can do except let them flow. I tighten my arms around Ryan and cry into his chest. I know I'm soaking his t-shirt with my tears and snot, but he doesn't seem to care as he strokes a hand up and down my back, trying to comfort me.

No one has ever held me in his arms while I cry. He's also whispering soothing things in my ear and somehow it's helping. With a half-sniffle, half-hiccup, I pull back and know I must look an absolute mess. I wipe my runny nose with the back of my hand. "Sorry about your shirt," I say, but he only shrugs.

"I don't care about my shirt," he says and brushes my hair back. "You wanna talk about it?"

God, those eyes of his suck me in and next thing I know, I'm spilling my guts. I've never told anyone about my parents dying or my uncle or the terrible things that he did. But, Ryan inspires trust and I know he won't tell anyone my dark secrets.

"After my parents died when I was 16, I moved in with my Uncle Wayne and Aunt Sylvia. I'd never been close to them, but I had nowhere else to go. They didn't pay much attention to me, but they fed and clothed me and sent me to school. They'd never had any children of their own."

I look down and see Ryan holds a lock of my hair, rubbing it between his fingers.

"Things weren't ever great, but they were bearable. At least until my aunt died. Then, my uncle turned mean. He drank all the time and lost his job. He turned all that pent-up anger on me."

Ryan is a good listener and finally emptying out all the horror that happened over the past year feels like such a weight off my shoulders.

"He started hitting me and I'd stay away as much as possible."

Ryan lets go of my hair and lightly touches the crescent-shaped scar at the corner of my eye, right above my cheekbone.

"He threw a bottle at me one night."

"Jesus."

I shrug. Getting hit with a beer bottle isn't the worst part of this story and I almost stop right there. But, one look into Ryan's concerned gaze and I keep going. For better or for worse, I tell him the part that I try to forget and lock deep down in my soul.

"My uncle has a lot of debt and he owed some guy a few grand. He was going to sell me to his friend for the night. Guess he figured my virginity would pay it off."

"Christ," Ryan hisses and everything about him darkens-- his eyes, face, energy.

"That's why I had to run away. No one is going to use my virginity and I'm never going back there. It's mine and I should be the one to choose who I give it to. And, I want the first man I sleep with to be gentle and kind. Not the highest bidder."

For a long moment, Ryan absorbs my story without a word. Then, he simply says, "Okay."

"Okay, what?" I ask, confused.

"I'll help you with your...request. At least if it's with me, I know it'll be a good experience for you."

My eyes widen.

"But, just the one time."

I don't have any words, can't believe that he's agreeing to take my virginity. I just nod.

"And, it can't be here. None of the residents can find out."

"Tonight?" I ask.

"Whenever you're ready."

"Tonight," I say. I'm not giving him any time to change his mind.

I feel like a horse chomping at the bit. I'm so ready to go, but Ryan tells me we'll leave in about half an hour. "Take a shower, get ready. Wear something special," he says.

*Special?* What does he mean? I don't have anything nice or fancy. I feel a wave of panic as I start to comb through the meager clothing in my drawers and closet. I end up choosing my nicest black bra and matching panties and a little sundress with flowers on it.

In exactly 30 minutes, I step out of my apartment and see him waiting by the pool, hands in his pockets, gaze on the water. My heart skips when I notice his thick, brown hair is damp from a shower. And, when I step up beside him, he smells so good. Like soap and fresh laundry and a hint of something spicy. Cologne, maybe? I bite my lip and think it's really cute that he wanted to get ready when he could've just pushed me up against a tree and been done with it.

I get the impression that it's really important to him to make this special for me. I have no idea why, but I appreciate the sweet gesture.

"Ready?" he asks.

His voice is husky and I know once we leave and get to the hotel that there's no turning back. For me, anyway. I have no doubt that Ryan would stop the moment I asked. "Ready," I say in as firm a voice as I can muster.

Ryan takes me to a well-known hotel chain that doesn't scream sleazy hook-up joint which I appreciate. It's quiet and there are a few other cars in the parking lot. I wait in his truck while he checks us in. God, I'm suddenly nervous. I wipe my sweaty palms down my dress and swallow hard.

I know I'm making the right decision and I know I've chosen the right man. But, still, I can't suppress the fluttery sensations in my stomach. I feel like I'm about to jump out of a plane and skydive or step off the end of a bridge and bungee jump into nothingness.

He returns a few minutes later and I get out. "Second floor, room 212," he says and we walk over to the staircase. He motions for me to head up first and I feel anxious and edgy. But, I push the feelings aside. I stop in front of room 212 and Ryan opens the door.

I step inside and flip on the light. There's one large bed in the middle of the room and I swallow down my nerves, trying to get them under control. *I want this*, I remind myself. I hear Ryan set his keys on the table and I can't seem to slow my rapid breathing.

"Hailey..."

I turn around and take a deep breath.

"If you've changed your mind-"

"No," I tell him and move closer. "I haven't." I reach out both hands and place them on his hard chest. I curl my fingers into his t-shirt and pull him to me. Then, Ryan leans down and captures my mouth in the best kiss I've ever received. His lips move over mine, slowly at first, but then something happens.

Something like an explosion.

Everything becomes hot and hazy and I lean into him as he angles his head over mine, deepening the kiss.

*Oh. My. God.*

I've never been kissed like this and when his tongue slides into my mouth, I tentatively answer back with mine, tasting him. My hands still clench his t-shirt and I let go and slide them up, my fingers slipping through the hair at the base of his neck. I like that it's a little too long and I circle my fingers through it.

After kissing me thoroughly, Ryan pulls back and his green eyes glow bright with desire. He wants me. Need is stamped all over his face and knowing this eases my nerves. He's not just doing me a favor. There's a hunger there and, together, we're going to satisfy it.

"If at any time you want to stop-"

"I won't," I interrupt.

"I want you to know that I will," he finishes.

"I know. I trust you, Ryan."

He gives a nod then cups my face and begins to kiss me again. My God, the man can kiss. He's very thorough and when his lips move down to my neck, I suck in a breath and my knees go weak.

"You taste so sweet," he murmurs, hands now on my hips, tongue leaving wet kisses down the curve of my throat. He pulls me closer, right up against him, and there's no mistaking the hardness pressing into me. A part of me freaks out a little and another, larger part of me gets excited.

His hands move down my hips, slip down to the hem of my dress and he fists the material. But, he doesn't pull it up any further, just licks up my jaw and kisses me again in that slow, deep, sensual way that's making me breathe harder.

I need more. When I slip my hands under his shirt and begin to trace the grooves of his six-pack abs, I feel him tense up. But, then, he takes a step back and whips the shirt off. "Go ahead," he says. "Touch me."

He's ripped and I let my hands explore the hard ridges of his stomach then move over to his rock-hard biceps where there's a tattoo of a pair of wings split by a dagger. The number "160" is inked right below the dagger's tip. I like it. A lot.

I also decide that I like touching his body. It's so warm and smooth, yet hard at the same time. I glide my hand back over and circle my fingertips lightly over his flat nipples.

"Can I taste you?" I ask.

His nostrils flare and he gives me a sharp nod. When I lean closer and trace my tongue over his clean skin, he sucks in a breath and drops his head back. His chest begins to rise and fall in jerky movements and it amazes me that I have this kind of effect on him.

When I pull back, he's staring at me and the intensity in those green eyes is deep and a little intimidating. Then, he reaches down, grasps the bottom of my dress and slips it up and over my head. I feel exposed and fight the urge to cover myself, but Ryan quickly makes me feel comfortable when he tells me how beautiful I am.

"Lay down," he says and I scoot back on the bed while he unbuttons, unzips and then drops his jeans to the floor. I can't help but look down and his boxer briefs look ready to burst. Ryan slides up over me and I let my nails trail down his smooth back.

His tongue flicks along my neck and then lowers. "You smell like vanilla ice cream. Taste like it, too." When his lips graze my breast, I let out a little gasp and arch beneath him.

"Funny," I say, struggling to breathe as his mouth covers my bra and sucks, "because your eyes are usually the color of mint chocolate chip ice cream."

He looks up at me. "Usually?"

"Now, they're darker like wet, green grass."

Somehow, my comment makes them turn another shade darker. I give a small whimper when he unsnaps my bra and tosses it aside. "You're perfect, Hailey," he murmurs, moving his mouth from one breast to the other, sucking and laving and making me squirm beneath him.

I feel his mouth move lower, lips tracing around my navel, and I suck in a breath, waiting to see what he does next. And, just when I'm about to burst from anticipation, Ryan drops his mouth over the front of my best black underwear and kisses me.

"Ohh," I moan as a fire stokes between my legs. He knows exactly what he's doing and I'm at his mercy. I feel his fingers slide beneath the elastic, slowly drag my panties down and then they wind up on the floor next to my bra.

When his mouth drops again, there's no barrier and I bite my lip hard as all these strange, exhilarating, pulsing feelings begin to fill me. He's licking and stroking and sucking and my hips buck up off the mattress. "Oh, my God," I say.

I think I feel him smile between my thighs, but I'm not sure. The only thing I'm sure of is his mouth is making a part of me come alive that I never knew existed. A pressure begins to build and it's intense and my breathing is all ragged and I don't know what to do. When I try to squeeze my thighs together, he pushes them further apart, lifts my hips up off the bed and sinks his face back down between my thighs. When he blows on me, I try to twist, but he holds me tight.

"Let go, sweetheart."

"I...can't," I say. Something is building, but I don't know what to do. Until one of his fingers slips inside me and his lips wrap around my clit and suck. *Holy hell.* My whole body vibrates and I thread my fingers through his hair and pull it hard. Wave after wave of pleasure rolls through me and I feel my body spasm.

My eyes slide shut and I feel like I'm floating as I sink into the softness of the bed. *Wow.* Ryan Fox has a mouth that knows how to please. I feel him move back up over me and I let out a content sigh. When I finally open my eyes, I see his mouth edge up.

"You like that?" he asks.

"Oh, yeah."

Pure, masculine pride fills his face and he leans down and kisses me. But, it's not slow like before. It's harder, more demanding and hotter. So very hot.

"Good," he says and moves between my legs. "Because we're just getting started."

*Oh, my goodness.* After that, I'm not sure how much more I can take.

# Chapter Eight: Ryan

*I honestly don't know how much more I can take,* I think. I haven't had sex in a very long time and Hailey is driving me into a frenzy. She's so damn responsive and all I want to do is slam into her and release this ache. But, I know I need to take it slow and be gentle.

And, I'm trying my damndest. But, it is not easy and takes every ounce of my self-control.

I slip a hand down between our bodies and she's dripping. "So wet," I whisper. This time, instead of one finger, I slide two into her body. *God, she's tight.* She pushes against my hand and I circle my thumb around her clit.

"Ryan," she cries.

"I'm right here. I've got you." Orgasm number two hits her hard and she's like a pile of jelly when I pull my hand back up. My cock throbs painfully and I can't wait any longer. I slip out of my boxer briefs and reach for the condom on the nightstand. I roll it on and look down into her glazed eyes.

"Hold on," I warn her. I plan to be as gentle as possible, but for fuck's sake, my dick is hard as steel and I have a feeling this could turn into a wild ride.

Hailey throws her arms around me and I move between her legs, weight on my elbows and hovering at her wet entrance, when she starts kissing my earlobe. *Fuck.* I'm literally going to explode, I think, as I grit my teeth and begin to push into her.

I feel her body tense and I freeze. "You're really, um, big," she says.

"Just relax," I say. I pull back out and then start to slide in again. Her body begins to loosen up more and I look into her big, brown eyes and thrust deep. I smother her cry with a kiss and pull her leg up higher, adjusting our position. Then, I start to move, trying to keep a slow, steady rhythm, but when she scratches her nails down my back and makes this sexy little mewling sound in the back of her throat, my control snaps.

Hailey wraps her legs around my waist and I pump my hips, driving into her tight, little body like a man who's possessed. Sensation overwhelms me and desire makes me lose my mind a little. She feels so fucking good and my hard kisses match my hard thrusts.

I reach down between us and stroke her. I need her to climax before me. This night is about her, not me. But, hell, I hope she gets there fast or that's not going to happen.

After a minute, she's writhing and arching and then her body trembles with release. *Good girl.* The pressure building at the base of my spine shatters and, with one final thrust, I explode with a loud groan. It's like the heavens open and angels serenade me. Nothing ever felt so fucking good.

I drop down beside her, breathing hard, and realize that this little virgin just made me come harder than I ever have before in my life. It catches me completely off-guard and I study her profile. She turns her head, chest still moving up and down hard, and gives me a crooked smile.

"Wow," she murmurs. "I didn't think it would be like that."

I reach out and gently push the hair back off her face. "Like what?" I ask.

"Like a lot of shooting stars all at once." I give her a quizzical look and she explains further. "Hot and bright and beautiful."

*Huh.* No one has ever described sex with me quite like that before. It's flattering. And, even though I had my doubts and plenty of misgivings at first, I'm glad I slept with her and was her first. I roll out of bed and get rid of the condom.

But, now it's over. No more, I remind myself.

Suddenly, I'm not so happy that I made that rule.

I have to think about Hailey, though. I don't want it to get around the complex where everyone knows that we're sleeping together. She doesn't deserve to have that kind of reputation because she's a good girl.

I get back in bed and pull the sheet up to my waist. "I'm glad you enjoyed it," I say.

"I more than enjoyed it." She traces a finger up my arm.

I reach over and grab her hand. "Hailey. One time. That was our agreement."

She pulls her hand away. "I know." She eyes me and then looks down and picks at the blanket. "I'm sorry if it wasn't that good for you, though."

"Why do you think it wasn't good for me?" I ask carefully. *Is she kidding?* She just rocked my fucking world. Tilted it completely off its axis.

"Because I didn't really, you know, do much back...for you."

"You were perfect."

She rolls her eyes. "You don't have to lie to try to make me feel better. I know I just laid there and let you do everything."

"Do you know how responsive you were? How passionate? I feel honored that you chose me and I just hope that I was good enough for you."

"You were more than good, Ryan." She looks down again, suddenly shy. "Honestly, I didn't think I was going to even like it."

"Why didn't you think you'd like it?"

Hailey lifts her hand and covers her face. "You're embarrassing me."

*God, she's adorable.* I pull her hand away from her red face and lace my fingers through hers. "It may have been your first time, but you didn't disappoint. You actually surprised me."

"I did? How so?"

"You're just very…refreshing."

"I just didn't want to disappoint you."

"Baby, I didn't want to disappoint you." I kiss the back of her hand and smile. "Taking someone's virginity is a lot of pressure."

"Have you before?"

"Slept with a virgin?" She nods. "The last time was when I was a virgin."

"Really?"

"We were both 17 and she was my first girlfriend."

"And, was it amazing?"

I burst out laughing. "No. It was bumpy and awkward and over in a couple of minutes."

Hailey smothers a laugh and I look down and realize I'm still holding her hand. And, it feels really good. Dare I say, right?

"Guess you've learned a few things over the years," she says in a low voice.

"A couple tricks, anyway."

"Have you been with a lot of women?"

I shift against the pile of pillows, not really wanting to talk about my sexual history, but what the hell. Hailey is now a part of that history and has a right to know, I suppose. "I don't think so, but I'm hardly a saint."

"Go on," she says.

"Well, there was Alyssa, my first girlfriend-"

"B and A?"

When I frown, her mouth tilts up. "Bumpy and awkward," she clarifies.

"Right," I say with a chuckle. "We eventually figured it out. That lasted a couple years and then I met Paige. We dated for a year, she got pregnant and we decided to get married." I don't know what possessed me to tell her about my ex-wife and daughter. "After my divorce, there have been a few more women, but nobody special."

"The girls say they never see you bring anybody home."

"Because I don't need everyone at Sunset Terrace to know who I'm sleeping with. I'm a little more discreet than that."

"Hence the hotel room," she says with a wave of her other hand.

"Exactly. It's no one's business." I finally slide my hand out of hers. "That's why this is going to remain our secret, right?"

She doesn't say anything for the longest time. Then, she finally utters a very unconvincing, "Sure."

"Hailey-"

But, she moves away from me, pulling the sheet with her, and swings her legs over the opposite side of the bed. Hailey stands up, reaches down and grabs her clothes off the floor. Laying there, naked and uncovered, I watch her head toward the bathroom.

I can't tell what's going on in that head of hers. Is she pissed? I just let her go and while she gets dressed, I do the same. We had a deal and now it's done.

*Time to go*, I tell myself as I zip my jeans up and pull my shirt over my head. I followed through, took her virginity like she wanted, and now it's over.

*Fuck*. There's a really big part of me that wants to drag her back under the covers with me and do it all over again. But, no, I can't think like that. It's dangerous.

When I pull my truck up alongside the building back at Sunset Terrace, right alongside my apartment, Hailey finally looks over at me. She didn't say a word the entire way back and I don't know what the hell to think.

"Thank you, Ryan," she whispers. Then, she opens the door and walks away.

I can't move, just watch the way her flowered dress swishes around her legs as she heads back over to her place. She looks so young and, despite just having had sex with me, completely innocent. I suck in a breath, pry my ass out of the car and look up at the dark sky above.

I don't think I'm going to be able to forget this night or Hailey Lane as easily as I'd hoped.

Back in my apartment, I drop down on the couch, pull out my cell phone and see I have two new messages. The first one is from Ryker Flynn, an old friend from when I was a Night Stalker. He was a Navy SEAL and is one of the best guys I know. I had the pleasure of flying him and his team on several missions. Now, he works at a security firm and has a new wife and baby daughter. Ryker says something about catching up and asks if I want to grab a beer with him and Griff, another one of the guys who works at Platinum Security.

It's late, so I'll text him back in the morning. It's been awhile so I look forward to catching up with him. I don't know Griff quite as well, but he's funny as hell and seems like a good guy.

When the other message plays, it's Bella and I sit up straighter.

*Hi, Dad. I know you wanted to see me and I'm free on Tuesday. You know, if you still want to meet up. If not, no big deal. Talk to you later.*

I play the message again and realize how much I miss my daughter. I haven't seen her in a couple of months and it feels like forever. And, even though it's after midnight, I text her back right away: *Yes, Tuesday sounds great. Look forward to seeing you and catching up. Love you.*

Bella hasn't told me that she loves me since she was probably about five. My heart twists up in my chest at the thought and I'd give anything to hear it. But, I'm always careful not to push her too hard. I know Paige blames me for our divorce and, in turn, so does Bella.

I'm the bad guy and I don't necessarily believe our failed marriage was one-hundred percent my fault, but I take on the majority of the burden for things not working out. I just don't want Paige talking shit about me to Bella.

The notion of having an estranged daughter kills me, but that's where we've somehow found ourselves. With every passing year, it feels like she's pulled further and further away from me. I understand that she has a busy life with work, school and friends, but I wish she would make time to see me more.

*Who am I kidding?*

I get the feeling that Bella would rather sit home and do nothing than spend time with her old man. But, that doesn't mean that I'm giving up on her. It just makes me want to work harder at improving our relationship.

And, I'm really hoping that our lunch this Tuesday is a step in the right direction.

*As long as she doesn't cancel,* I think. Because, unfortunately, she tends to do that an awful lot.

# Chapter Nine: Hailey

The next morning, I lay in my bed and think about last night with Ryan. It was perfect, but the thing is, I don't want it to be over. I stretch my arms above my head and feel an ache between my legs. It's a pleasant reminder of everything he did to me.

I know we agreed that it would only be one time and I'm usually very good about keeping my promises. But, the more I think about it, the more I'm convinced that this isn't the best decision. For either of us.

Ryan Fox is playing it safe. For some reason, I scare him. I'm not sure if it's because I'm so much younger or what, but he's putting his head before his heart. I just know it.

My heart feels a connection to him. It has since the moment he helped me carry that heavy box of books into my place when I was moving in. I feel myself falling for the quiet, strong mysterious man who lives in apartment 7. But, I'm not quite sure what to do about it.

All I know is that I want to know everything about him. He confided a few personal things in me last night, but there's so much that I don't know. Simple things like his favorite food and color and season. I want to know what movies he likes and what foods he enjoys. More than anything, I want to feel his strong arms around me again as he kisses me senseless.

Ryan is an amazing kisser. He does other things pretty damn well, too. I wasn't expecting to ever enjoy sex after my uncle revealed his plans to sell my virginity. That's why I knew I had to find someone who would be sweet and take his time. Ryan was literally the perfect choice. He introduced me to a whole level of pleasure that I hadn't known before. We connected last night on a physical and emotional level. If I felt it then he had to have, too. I hope, anyway.

I'm not giving up on him. But, I need advice because I have no experience with this kind of thing. The last thing I want to do is come off like some kind of stalker and scare him away further. I need to talk to someone who has more experience with men and relationships and the first person who comes to mind is Jasmine Torres.

I hop out of bed, a plan forming, and wash up and get dressed. Then, I head next door. I am bound and determined to get under Ryan's skin like he's gotten under mine.

I knock on Jasmine's door and she opens it a minute later looking like she just dragged herself out of bed. She looks sleep-rumpled, but gorgeous. "What time is it?" she asks and yawns behind a hand.

"Almost 11," I say.

"You interrupted my beauty sleep," she says and throws the door open. "What's up, Indiana?"

"I'm sorry. I just, ah, needed some advice."

Jasmine lights up and motions for me to sit on the couch. I can tell that she loves giving advice and playing mother hen. "Let me just brush my teeth, make some tea and then we can chat. What is it about? Boy trouble already?"

"Yeah, you can say that."

"Well, you definitely came to the right person," she says and heads into the kitchen. "You like tea?" she calls out.

"Sure," I say.

A few minutes later, she hands me a steaming mug of green tea, sits beside me and curls her long legs beneath her. "Okay, spill it. Who's caught your eye?"

I let out a long breath and stare down into the mug. "Ryan," I murmur.

She gives me a blank look then her almond eyes widen. "Foxy Flyboy?" she practically screeches. "You like Foxy Flyboy!"

"Shh," I say. My luck, the whole complex just heard her yell that and I cringe.

"Sorry," she says and drops her voice. "But, this is unbelievable. Okay, why Ryan? What's going on? Does he like you, too? Did something happen between the two of you? Oh, my God, tell me right now!"

Her barrage of questions makes me nervous. "Okay, first of all, calm down, please. You're giving me anxiety." She nods and sits up straighter waiting for me to continue. "I'm not sure where exactly to start, but since day one, I felt a connection, a spark, with him. But, he pushed me away and didn't want anything to do with it."

"Yeah, that's Ryan. Always putting himself last." She blows on her tea.

"Well, um, last night, he and I-"

Jazz's mouth drops open. "What happened?"

"I needed help with something and he...helped me."

"Help with what?"

I shift, suddenly uncomfortable. "Losing my virginity," I say in a low voice.

"Holy shit! You and Foxy Flyboy did the no pants dance? And, he was your *first*? This is epic!"

I feel my face heat up in embarrassment and begin to wonder if I shouldn't have told her. "You're not going to tell anyone, right? Because Ryan doesn't want anyone else to know."

"My lips are sealed," she says and makes a motion of locking them and throwing away the key. "But, it's not like y'all can keep something like this a secret forever. People are going to see you sneaking back and forth to his place."

"Well, that's the thing. We both agreed that it would be a one-time deal."

"And, now you're having second thoughts about that?"

"Exactly."

"Well, what are you really feeling? Do like him because he was your first or because you feel a deeper pull. Like he's the one you could spend the rest of your life with?"

"There's an attraction there that I can't ignore. And, I'm pretty sure he feels it, too."

"Okay, so Ryan needs to man-up and face his feelings."

"How do I get him to do that?" I ask and lean forward.

Jasmine sighs. "It's not going to be easy. Especially with him. He's really private and probably takes things like sex extremely seriously. Though, I get the feeling he knows how to show a girl a good time between the sheets. Am I right?"

I flush. "I mean, I don't have anything to compare it to, but...yeah, he was really, really good."

She gives me a smile. "I knew it. He has this vibe about him. That he knows how to get things done. Are you still tingly?" I nod and she claps her hands in delight. "This is great. The non-virgins are finally starting to outnumber the virgins in this complex."

"Who else is?" I ask, suddenly curious.

"Savannah was til Nick. And, Taylor, too. I'm not sure about Morgan, though, because she never talks about it. When sex comes up, she always deflects and changes the subject. She's really mysterious about it."

"I haven't even seen her around yet."

"Yeah, she's like a ghost, but I love her to death. She's just always caring for her mom or working. Poor girl needs to get away and forget everything. But, back to you and Ryan. Hmm."

Jasmine takes a sip of her tea, thinking, and I ask her what else she knows about him.

"Not a lot," she says. "Like I mentioned before, I've lived here three years and I've never seen him with a woman."

A part of me is a little glad to hear that, but I wonder why. "He told me he hasn't been serious with anyone really since his divorce. Why don't you think he dates?"

She shrugs. "He might, he might not. Who really knows? He's so private. I mean, he could be a serial killer and have a woman chained up in his place and we'd never know."

"Oh, God, don't say that."

Jazz laughs. "I'd be the neighbor they'd interview who said how shocked I am because he seemed like such a nice guy."

"He is not a serial killer," I say and roll my eyes. "Have you ever seen his ex-wife?"

She shakes her head. "Nope. Haven't seen his daughter either, but I think she's around our age because he once mentioned something about her taking classes. I just assumed she was in college."

"He said they had her when he was only 20."

"Really?" She eyes me. "So, you guys actually talked, too."

I nod. "A little."

When I look up, Jasmine is studying me. "Here's what I think-- you should go for it. If he's going to pretend to be noble and keep the bargain of only one time then make him realize what a dumb idea that is. From what I've seen, Ryan is a lonely, unhappy man who deserves to have some love and happiness in his life. If you can give that to him then you will have everyone's blessing here, especially mine."

An excited feeling fills me. "What should I do, though? How do I make him see that I could be really good for him?"

"Go seduce him."

"What? I don't know how and-"

"Hailey, you slept with the man last night. Unless he was a complete robot, you should've picked up on a few things. Like what he likes, what turns him on, what drives him crazy. Use those things to weaken his resolve."

"I don't know if I can do that."

"I have faith in you," she says and then stands up. "My flight to New York is in a couple of hours so I need to get ready. But, promise you'll keep me updated."

"It's like I'm on a mission now," I say with a little smile.

"Operation: Fucking Foxy Flyboy."

"Oh, my God." I bury my face in my hands and she bursts out laughing.

Back at my place, I see a message on my phone and listen to it. My mouth drops when it's someone from the Magnolia Club and they invite me to perform there next Saturday night. With a scream, I jump up on my couch and bounce around like a crazy person. I'm so excited and the first person that I want to tell is Ryan.

It gives me a good reason to go over there. But, not until tonight. Jazz said to seduce him and I want to do this right. I start thinking of all the things I could do and then decide on how to kick off Operation: Fucking Foxy Flyboy.

It's going to be a risk and may not work, but if he's attracted to me then that'll give me the boost of confidence I need. I check the time and it's barely noon. Operation: Triple F won't happen until later tonight, so I have all day to prepare. And, the first thing I need is a new bathing suit.

I go out shopping and pick up a cute, little black two-piece. It's not too skimpy or daring, but it shows off enough skin that it should get Ryan's motor revving. I plan to lounge by the pool today, in plain view of his kitchen window, and want him to notice. I hope that he can't help but watch me lay in a lounge chair all afternoon with my straps down and my body glistening with oil.

Two hours later, I stretch out on my towel-covered chair and glance over at Ryan's window. I've been out here an hour and there's been no sign of him. I sigh. I know he's home because his truck is still parked along the side of the building where he left it after we got back from the hotel last night.

He's usually out and about during the day so it's strange that I haven't seen him yet. Just as I'm thinking this, his door opens and he steps out. And, he looks straight at me. I feel a surge of triumph pass through me and I know he can't see me watching him behind my sunglasses. But, I am completely aware of his every move.

He looks good in a navy t-shirt and worn jeans and I see him head over to the small shed on the opposite side of the pool. He goes inside and then reappears with a couple buckets of some chemicals. I pretend not to notice as he approaches, but when he's close enough, I lift my hand and wave.

Ryan sets the buckets down at the edge of the pool and moves closer to me. "Hi. How are you?" he asks.

His gaze skims down me and I sit up and cross my ankles. "Good. A little sore."

Heat flashes through his green eyes and he stares at where my straps hang down my arms. "Guess that's to be expected."

"I like it, though. It's like I can still feel you inside me." Even though I want to pull my straps back up, I don't. *Let him get a good look,* I think.

He hisses in a breath and those eyes darken. "Hailey. Don't say that."

"Why not?"

"Someone might hear."

I shrug. "I don't care."

"You should. You don't want to get a bad reputation."

We both look up when Mason and Cody's door slams open and their loud voices float down. They've got surfboards tucked under their arms and they start down the stairs from the second-floor apartment they share. When they head in our direction, Ryan picks up a bucket of chemicals and tosses them in the pool.

"Hey, Ryan, this idiot poured grease down the garbage disposal again and now it's all jacked up," Mason says. They're both shirtless and wear board shorts and flip flops. As cute as they are, Ryan is the only one I'm yearning to have.

Cody slugs his arm. "Dude, I forgot."

"Guys, that will clog it every time," Ryan says.

"Can you fix it?" Mason asks. "Sorry this guy's such a moron."

"I'm not a plumber, bro. How am I supposed to know what can and cannot go down a drain?"

"Grease can't," Ryan says in a dry voice.

"Sorry. I won't forget again."

"Yes, you will," Mason says.

"Hey, Hailey. Catchin' some rays?" Cody asks with a grin. "Just let us know when you're ready to catch some waves and we'll take you out surfing."

"Thanks, guys," I say and give them a little wave.

As they walk away, it looks like Ryan frowns. But, he quickly masks the sour look on his face and turns his attention back to the pool.

"What are you doing?" I ask when he tosses some stuff into it.

"Shocking the pool."

He sounds grumpy and I bite back a smile. "What's that?"

"Raising the chlorine level quickly."

"Why?"

"So, you don't have to swim in a pool full of algae," he snaps.

*Wow. Someone is being awfully snippy.* I stretch and finally pull my straps back up. His gaze flickers to my bikini top and then moves away. "Something wrong?" I ask, all innocence.

"No," he grumbles and finishes with the chemicals.

"Ryan?"

"Huh?"

"Do you like my new bathing suit?"

A muscle flexes in his jaw. "Stop it."

I smile. "I'm just asking. I almost got the string bikini, but was scared it would accidentally come untied if I went swimming." I slide off the lounge chair and he freezes when I move up beside him. "It's hot. You should take a dip."

"I'm fine," he grits out.

"Are you?" I ask in a playful voice. My gaze dips down and, if I'm not mistaken, his jeans are looking a little snug.

Before I can say another word to torment him, Ryan snatches the buckets up and stomps back over to the shed. He stows them and then heads back to his place where he slams the door shut behind him.

*Hmm.* Part one of my plan just went off without a hitch. Tonight, it will be time to activate part two and make Ryan want me so badly that he can't see straight.

# Chapter Ten: Ryan

With thoughts of Hailey laying by the pool in her two-piece dancing in my head, I trip over the edge of a surfboard in Cody and Mason's messy apartment. *Goddammit.* I rub my hurt toe and swear again.

I think she's trying to get under my skin. It's like she's purposely trying to rile me up and I don't appreciate it. We agreed on one time. And, yes, okay, I'm starting to regret that decision. But, I can't break my promise. If I slept with her again, it wouldn't be good for either of us.

Technically, it would be amazing. But, I'm trying to think long-term and trying to protect her. I keep trying to convince myself that she would be better off with someone like Cody or Mason, but just the thought pisses me off.

I want her with me.

*Dammit.*

If her goal is to get me all hot and bothered, then congratulations. *You did it, Hailey.* I feel all out of sorts and even though my mind keeps warning me to stay the hell away from her, my body is ready for round two.

As soon as I finish cleaning the grease out of the garbage disposal, I'm meeting Bella for dinner. I'm looking forward to it and I hope that things go well between us. I even have a birthday gift for her and I hope she likes it.

Fifteen minutes before we're supposed to meet, I sit down on a bench outside the trendy vegan restaurant on La Cienega. Bella told me she's been a vegan for the past few months so I checked online and this place got pretty high reviews. I hope she likes it.

I look down at the carefully wrapped gift on my lap and hope she likes this, too. I wandered around the mall for almost two hours last week, at a complete loss, and really wanted to get her something thoughtful. Not just a candle or shower gel or perfume. I ended up deciding on a really fancy chess set. I remember she'd been really into playing chess a couple years ago and I thought that she'd appreciate it.

Then, I got nervous it wouldn't be right and stopped in a jewelry store. I picked out a delicate gold necklace with a little heart dangling from it. I've always heard that you can't go wrong with jewelry.

*God, I'm nervous.* I realize my leg is bouncing up and down and I stop it. I watch people go in and out of the restaurant and wait patiently. Unlike me, Bella is always late. As a Night Stalker, we couldn't be late. Our missions were on short notice and ever since, I'm always early for everything.

But, at 6pm, a half an hour after we're supposed to meet, I begin to wonder if she's going to even show up. I check my phone for the twentieth time, but no text. I pull her name up, tell her I'm here and ask if she's running late.

A minute later, my phone beeps. I open her text: *Oh, no. So sorry, but I completely forgot. Can we reschedule?*

I drop my head back against the building and sigh. *She forgot?* I'm glad that I rank so high in her life that she didn't even remember we made plans to meet today. I feel like an asshole and even more so, a bad father.

This is all my fault. If I had focused more on our relationship when she was younger instead of my military career, I know we'd be closer right now. I suppose that I deserve this. It still hurts, though.

I text her back: *Sure. How about tomorrow?*

Her cool response comes a few seconds later: *Let me check my schedule and I'll get back to you.*

I know exactly what that means. It means I'm going to have to change the birthday wrapping paper on this gift to Christmas paper.

I pull myself up from the bench and head back to my truck.

Back at Sunset Terrace, I park alongside the building, turn the car off and sit there for a long time. I think about Bella and how I'd give anything to mend our relationship. It literally makes my heart break to know that I have a daughter who doesn't give a shit about me.

I just wish I could figure out what the hell to do to make things better. I know that I need to give her space and time, but a part of me wonders if that's for the best. I feel her drifting further away.

I finally get out of the car and walk around the corner to my place. My gaze moves over the now-quiet pool where Hailey tormented me earlier to her apartment where a light brightens the window. I need to stop obsessing over her and figure out how to make things right with my daughter.

After shutting the door behind me, I toss the birthday present on a nearby table and head straight for the fridge and an ice-cold beer. Time to drown my sorrows. I twist the cap off and then drop down in my chair, take a long sip, but don't bother to turn the TV on. I just want to sit here and be miserable.

Beside me, my open laptop dings. I roll my head over and look where it sits on the couch. With a long-suffering sigh, I reach over and drag it onto my lap to check my email. I haven't checked lately and I'm sure there's a ton of junk mail to delete.

I pull my new mail up and do a double take. There are at least 50 emails from the dating site. *What the hell?* I open the first one and it's from Beth. Her profile picture shows that she's a cute blonde sitting up on a horse. I open her message: *Hi, Ryan- it's so nice to meet you. I love your pic and would love to get to know you even more. Maybe you could take me flying?*

*Flying?* Oh, yeah, I forgot that I posted a picture of me from my Night Stalker days. I'm thinking how I should respond back, but then decide I should read through all of the messages first and see if anyone strikes me as someone I'd like to get to know better.

I've never had so many women show this much interest in me and it's kind of flattering. It's probably just because I'm in my uniform in the picture. Women like men in uniform. Or, so I've heard.

*Whatever.* At this point, the messages help boost my mood. Some of them are sweet and flirty while others are just downright dirty. I delete the crude ones and focus on the more serious ones where the women seem to actually want to get to know me and not just have a one-night stand.

Ding. Ding. Ding.

*Shit, I just got three new ones.* They're coming in faster than I can sort through them. And, I'm not going to lie. It feels pretty damn good. I spend the next few hours checking out the messages, women's profiles and do some googling on them, too.

In the end, I find myself especially interested in a woman named Daphne. She's divorced and a graphic designer close to my age with a 20-year old daughter. Her dark hair is shoulder-length and she appears fit and has a nice smile. I decide I'm going to message her back. *Why the hell not? Isn't that why I did this in the first place? To try and meet a nice woman?*

Actually, I did it to get laid, but it would be nicer to find someone I had things in common with and to share my life with, right? I ask Daphne a little more about herself, finish my beer and glance down at my rugged watch. I can't believe it's almost midnight.

And, that's when I hear the knock on my door.

With a frown, I set my laptop aside and stride over to open it. Hailey stands there in a tank top and shorts. Her long dark hair hangs loose around her gorgeous face and she gives me a tentative smile.

"I know it's late," she says, "but, I saw your light still on and I wanted to invite you to a gig I booked. It's next Saturday at the Magnolia Club."

"That's really great," I say. "Congratulations."

"Thanks. I, ah, also wanted to apologize for earlier today. I'm sorry if I made you uncomfortable."

My heart rate increases exponentially and suddenly everything that we did the other night begins to play out in my head like a movie on the big screen. Every kiss, every touch, every time I thrust inside of her. I swallow hard and hear my laptop ding.

"I wanted to ask you for some advice, actually. Can I come in?"

I hesitate. I should be thinking about Darla, I mean Daphne, and possibly pursuing something with her, but this little girl in front of me is the one I want. I'm probably going to regret doing so, but I push the door wider and motion for her to come inside.

Hailey lets out a small sigh and looks up at me with those big, brown eyes that make me think of melted Hershey kisses. "What's going on?" I ask.

"This is kind of embarrassing, but I don't think we thought things through as thoroughly as we should have the other night."

My heart sinks. *Ah, fuck, she regrets it.* I don't know why exactly, but the idea that Hailey is having doubts about choosing me as her first upsets me. Maybe after having time to think things through, she feels like she made a mistake. Maybe I didn't live up to her expectations.

Maybe we should've done it again.

I clear my throat. "Are you...disappointed?"

Her eyes widen. "No. Not at all. What I mean is we agreed to only be together one time. And, I'm beginning to think that was a bit of a hasty decision because…"

I wait for her to continue, pulse pounding, knowing exactly what she's about to say.

"Because I haven't been able to stop thinking about you, Ryan. And, once wasn't enough."

*Fuck.* Without giving myself time to think, I yank her into my arms, crushing her against my chest. My mouth slams down and moves over hers with a desperateness that leaves us both breathless and panting.

"I haven't been able to stop thinking about you, either," I admit. I shouldn't be telling her this, knowing that I should keep my distance, but I can't. I run a hand through her hair and slant my head down to capture her lips again. All the slow gentleness from our first time together is gone and the gnawing hunger in my gut makes me rougher. My tongue plunges into her mouth and I push her back and down onto the couch. My laptop slides off the cushion and hits the carpeted floor with a dull thud.

As I stretch out over her body, she wraps her arms around my neck, arching beneath me, returning my heated kisses with just as much passion. Propped on my elbows, I drop my head and leave a trail of wet kisses down her silky neck. She wraps her legs around me, lifts her hips and I reach down and slide my hand down the front of her tiny shorts and into her panties.

*Holy shit.* She's dripping and I stroke my fingers up and down her slit, coaxing her legs apart further. A moan spills from her throat and I slowly circle her throbbing clit.

"Ryan," she murmurs, and her hips buck against my hand. "It's too good."

"You're so wet for me," I say in a raspy voice. I keep rubbing and stroking, working her until she's crying out. "That's right, baby girl. Let go." I look down into her dark eyes and slide two fingers up inside her slick passage. Her eyes slide shut as I move my fingers in and out and keep pushing against her with my thumb. "Come for me, Hailey. Come right on my hand."

"Oh, God," she cries and tightens around my fingers. I can feel her lower body spasm and her nails dig into my shoulders. She lets out a long moan and shudders from her head down to her toes. I pull my hand out of her pants and her eyes flutter open.

"Is this all for me, Hailey?" I ask and show her my glistening hand.

"Every last drop," she says.

I put my fingers in my mouth and suck them clean. The look on her face is priceless and I kiss her hard, sliding my tongue against hers, circling my rock-hard erection between her legs.

"I want you to teach me more," she whispers. "I want you to be the father I lost." She undulates her hips, grinding her hot, wet center against my cock. "I want you to show me, Daddy."

"*Fuck*," I hiss. How the hell am I supposed to say no to that? All rational thought goes out the window and all I can think about is being inside her again. "Gimme a sec," I rasp and struggle up. My mind is hazy as I head down to the nightstand drawer in my bedroom and grab a condom.

I'm not going to think too hard about this right now. I'm just going to give us both a lot of pleasure and worry about the consequences later. My stupid laptop dings a couple more times and when I return to the living room, Hailey is sitting up and my computer is on her lap.

"You're talking to women online?" she asks.

I can't miss the hurt in her voice. *Ah, shit.* "It's just a dating site I was on."

"Was? Because someone named Daphne has sent you three messages in the last 15 minutes."

I grab the damn laptop and drop it down on the chair. "I don't care about that," I tell her. I just want to take up where we left off, but her complete demeanor has changed.

"I care," she whispers.

"Goddammit." I sit down next to her, wishing I could turn it off as quickly as her. But, my cock is ready and raring to go and I shift on the couch, trying to find a degree of comfort. "Look, I thought meeting someone else would help me forget about you."

When I see the look on her face, I know that was the wrong thing to say.

"You wanted to forget about me?"

"Yes! God, ever since you moved in here, you've been driving me fucking crazy parading around in those little shorts and your bathing suit and flirting with me. I know we shouldn't be together, but it's like all you do is tempt me day and night. And, I'm so fucking weak, Hailey." I suck in a breath and she just blinks, absorbing my words. I look down at the condom in my hand and then toss it on the coffee table when my laptop dings again.

Hailey stands up and sniffs. "Daphne sent you another message."

"Hailey-"

She stops at the door and glances over her shoulder at me. "I thought you were different. I'm sorry for bothering you, Ryan. It won't happen again."

I jump up and jog over to the door, but she's gone and walking fast back to her place. I let out a long, frustrated sigh and drop my head against the doorframe.

Even though this is what I wanted-- to forget Hailey and focus on a woman more my age-- I feel like an asshole.

And, I have a feeling I just fucked everything up royally.

# Chapter Eleven: Hailey

*I feel like such a complete idiot,* I think as I hurry away from Ryan's apartment and back to my place. I can feel tears burning the back of my eyes and I just want to throw myself into bed and cry.

"Hailey?"

My head snaps up and I notice Taylor on the sidewalk. *Oh, no.* I wonder if she saw me leave Ryan's? She's dressed up in her club gear and must've just finished dancing at Club Noir. "Hey," I say in a shaky voice and swipe at my nose.

"Were you just at Ryan's?"

"Um…" *Shit.* I don't know what to say. So, I don't say anything and instead burst into tears.

"Oh, Hailey, what's wrong?" She walks over and concern laces her voice. "Do you wanna talk about it?

I nod and push my door open. I never thought Ryan would hurt me like this. I thought he was one of the good guys and would protect me. I sit on the couch and wipe the tears away. Taylor lets me finish crying and then reaches out and touches my arm.

"What's going on?"

I sniffle, not sure how to begin, but I think she already has a good idea of what's going on.

"You and Ryan?" she asks. I bite my lip and nod. "I kind of had a feeling."

"Really?"

"I saw the way you two kept looking at each other that day at the pool."

"I thought he cared," I say.

Taylor lets out a long sigh. "They all make you think that they care. Even nice guys like Ryan."

I hear bitterness in her voice and wonder who burned her? "Nobody else knows about us-- except Jasmine-- so I'd appreciate it if you would keep it quiet."

"Of course."

"This is all my fault. I practically begged him to sleep with me. And, I just found out he's talking to other women online."

"Really? Ryan doesn't seem like the type to do online dating."

"I saw the messages. I know we agreed to only one time, but he was my first, Taylor. I didn't expect to keep thinking about him. To want more."

"How did this even happen?"

"All I know is there's a spark between us. From the moment we met. And, all I wanted was for him to be my first. To take care of me. I convinced him, but then started to fall for him. Hard."

"Oh, sweetie, I'm sorry."

"When I went over there tonight, everything began happening again. And we almost-" my voice trails off and Taylor just nods. "But, then I heard his email keep dinging and some chick named Daphne was sending him all these messages."

"What do you even know about her? Have they even met in person?"

I shrug. "I don't know."

"I'm going to be honest. I have never seen Ryan with a woman. He's extremely discreet, but at the same time, I think he's just a really lonely man. I get the feeling he hasn't dated anyone seriously since his divorce. He's also a really stand-up guy. So, if he slept with you, I think that means something on his end."

"You do?"

"If he didn't feel anything, I think he'd stay away. Especially since, well, you're so much younger. Knowing Ryan, I wouldn't be surprised if he feels guilty about being with someone his daughter's age."

*I want you to show me, Daddy.*

I start to second-guess that Daddy comment. But, then I remember his response and I don't think he minded. At all.

"I don't know what to do," I say and run a hand through my hair.

"Do you really care about him?"

I nod. "So much."

"Then, I think you should give him the benefit of the doubt. The man is hardly a serial dater and is always by himself. If he's talking to someone online, it's probably new."

"Maybe."

"I say if you want him then go get him. Foxy Flyboy could use a little happiness in his quiet life."

I give Taylor a small smile. Maybe she's right.

After Taylor leaves, I curl up in my chair by the window and sing. It's the one thing that lets me go inside of myself and find peace. It allows me to shut everything else out and just be in the moment without any fear or uncertainty or unhappiness. It's a respite from my problems and daily life. Above all, it allows me to block out the pain and transport myself to another place.

Music is my savior.

The next morning, I think about everything that happened with Ryan and then I remember Taylor's advice. I don't know if she's right or if he actually cares, but I'm going to set everything aside for now and focus on the reason I'm here. To be a singer.

I'm excited that I booked a gig at the Magnolia Club, but there are a thousand more places in this city that I should go visit, introduce myself and drop off a demo CD. The more exposure I can get and the more people I meet, the better.

With those thoughts in my head, I set out and pound the pavement. I probably visit 20 places and make a few potential connections. Some booking agents are really friendly and take my demo and others act like they don't have time and direct me to their website with instructions on how to book a gig properly.

As daunting as it is and despite the overwhelming competition, I am not going to give up. Singing is the one thing that I am good at doing. It's the talent I was blessed with and now I need to figure out a way to let people hear me.

I've posted videos online and decide that I should probably do a new one. I haven't put one up in a few weeks and followers are fickle and lose interest fast if you don't keep things new and fresh. I want to do something cool so I head over to Lake Hollywood Park. I follow my GPS, drive around the mountain bend and follow the residential road that climbs above the Hollywood Reservoir.

I did some research online when I was in Indiana and seeing the Hollywood sign is something that I wanted to do. It would be the perfect place to record myself for a new video. When I reach the park, I pull up and park at the curb. It's not overly crowded which is nice and I hop out of my old truck.

*There it is*, I think, and look up at the iconic sign that has welcomed and spurned so many dreamers. The famous letters sit high up on the hillside and I walk a little closer, searching for the perfect spot.

Off to the side, beneath a tree, I pull up the video on my phone and hit record. I already know I'm going to sing two songs. One for fun and one that I'm actually feeling to the depths of my soul.

The first is a popular Miley Cyrus song about moving to L.A. I sing the fluffy words about hopping off the plane at LAX with a dream and my cardigan. After I finish "Party in the USA," I take a deep breath and launch into "Darn That Dream," another Billie Holiday favorite of mine.

"Darn that dream, I dream each night. You say you love me and hold me tight. But when I awake, you're out of sight. Oh, darn that dream." My voice sounds haunted, almost eerie to my own ears, but I keep singing.

"Darn your lips and darn your eyes. They lift me high above moonlit skies…"

The words pour forth, directly from my heart, out of my mouth and to the world. I lose myself in the melody and vocals. The song requires a fair amount of study and preparation before you can start improvising. But, I've been singing it for years and it flows easily and sounds pure.

"Darn that one track mind of mine. It can't understand that you don't care…Darn that dream and bless it, too. Without that dream I never would have you. But it haunts me and it won't come true. Oh, darn that dream."

When I hear a smattering of applause, I open my eyes and realize a few people have stopped to listen. I feel a blush warm my cheeks and I smile. "Thanks," I say and give a little courtesy.

"You should be on The Voice," someone says.

I chuckle and hit stop on the camera. Singing always lifts me up and makes me feel better. Some people meditate or do yoga to find balance and that zen place within, but I just need a song. Feeling renewed, I head back to my truck.

By the time I get back to Sunset Terrace, the sun is getting low and the day is winding down. I notice some people sitting in chairs by the pool and, as I get closer, I see it's Ryan and a couple of friends. *Hot* friends. When I pass by, Ryan and I make eye contact, but neither of us says a word.

Yet, something passes between us.

*Hmm*. This may be an opportunity to get him riled up and as I debate what to do, I see Jasmine and another girl peering out her window at the trio of male deliciousness. I walk over and wave. Jazz throws the door open and motions for me to come inside.

"Hurry up," she whispers.

"What's going on?" I ask as she pulls me through the door and shuts it fast.

"We're ogling Ryan's friends. C'mon." Jasmine motions to a dark-haired girl with stunning blue eyes. "Morgan, Hailey. Hailey, Morgan."

"Nice to meet you," I say.

"You, too," she says. "I live over in #2."

I move up beside them, look out the kitchen window above the sink and shake my head. "You know they can see you, right?" I ask.

"Shut. Up." Jazz is horrified.

I chuckle. "Yep." Then, I turn and move away to sit down at the kitchen table.

"Are you sure?" Morgan asks and moves back a bit.

"If I saw you then they did, too."

"Damn it," Jasmine turns and hops up on the counter. "Oh, well. They have to know what a commotion they're causing among the single Sunset Terrace ladies."

"Except for Ryan, though, I don't think they're single," Morgan says. "Look. They're both wearing wedding bands."

Jazz and I exchange a look, but she doesn't say anything.

"Who are they?" I ask.

"The big, muscular dream is Ryker, a friend from the military. And, I have no idea who the Hemsworth/Pine hybrid is, but, *daaaamn*, he's yummy."

I laugh at Jasmine's description and settle back in the chair. As good-looking as Ryan's buddies are, I only have eyes for him. Suddenly, I stand up, determined to make some waves. "Ladies, I'm feeling a little warm." They exchange looks as I head toward the door to leave. "I think it's time for a dip in the pool."

"Oh, shit," I hear Jasmine say behind me.

# Chapter Twelve: Ryan

I sit by the pool with Ryker Flynn and Griff Lawson and I'm glad they came by tonight to share a couple of beers and catch up. They both work for Jax Wilder over at Platinum Security, a firm that offers a variety of services from investigating and troubleshooting to personal bodyguards. They also have the ability to take care of other more shady jobs. The group is made up of former cops, CIA agents, ex-military and hackers so I have no doubt that they are a talented and deadly group.

But, right now, the former Navy SEAL and ex-CIA agent look far from fierce as they talk about their wives. Ryker can't stop gushing about Avery and their new daughter Luka while Griff, recently married to Lexi, announced that he's going to be a proud papa early next February.

I've known Ryker for a long time, since our days when I'd fly him into missions, and he's never looked happier. At 6'4" with short dark hair and the same rock-hard, military fit body he had when he was a SEAL, my friend went through some dark shit when he lost his entire team on a mission in the Columbian jungle. None of us were able to pull him back off the ledge or help ease his PTSD. Until Avery. She swept back into his life with a vengeance and made him want to live again.

And, I've only known Griffin Lawson about a year and the guy's a trip. With brown hair and sky blue eyes that make the ladies swoon, he looks like he should be an actor. I don't know a lot about his past as an agent, but I get the feeling he has some dark secrets, too. But, he hides them well behind an enormous amount of charm, humor and charisma.

These two are lucky, I think. They've overcome a lot of demons and found amazing women who they're starting families with and they have a job at Platinum Security that they love. I'm happy they've found their "happily-ever-afters," but I'm not going to lie.

I feel a bit envious.

To be honest, after Paige and I divorced, I never thought I'd get married again. But seeing how these two glow when they talk about their wives makes me wonder if I would do it all over again.

If I found the right woman, I think. I immediately think of Hailey and something low and hot tugs in my belly. When she walked by earlier, I wanted to grab her and pull her down onto my lap. Instead, our gazes connected briefly and she kept going.

I feel like I'm really screwing things up. Even worse than they were before and I don't know how to fix it.

"You've been single too long, Fox. What about you?" Ryker asks.

"What about me?" I ask with a wary expression.

"No one special?"

"Oh, Jesus, you're not turning into one of those guys, are you?"

"What do you mean?" Ryker asks.

"Now that you've found love and marriage, you want it for everyone else."

Ryker and Griff exchange a look. "All I'm saying is if I knew then what I know now, I wouldn't have fought it so hard."

"And, this guy fought it for about ten years," Griff adds with a chuckle.

Ryker lifts his middle finger and flips Griff off. "Yeah? Well, you got taken down in about a week, loverboy."

Griff tosses his middle finger right back. "What can I say? When you know, you know. And, I found out I have a weakness for redheads."

"I don't know," I say and lean back in my chair. "I've steered clear of serious relationships since my divorce."

"She wasn't the right one," Ryker says simply. As though that explains it all.

"I know exactly what you mean," Griff says and pops a stick of gum into his mouth. "I used to avoid relationships like the plague."

"So, what made it different?" I ask. I'm curious how these two went from perpetual bachelors to head over heels.

For a moment neither says anything. Then, Griff clears his throat and shrugs. "Lexi made it different. She challenged me in every way and was the biggest pain in my ass." We laugh. "But, I loved it and when I thought about the case ending and us going our separate ways, it literally made me panicky. I knew I wanted her in my life all the time."

"Awwwww," Ryker and I say together in a teasing tone.

I think Griff flushes before he grumbles a curse. Then, he turns his attention to Ryker. These two love throwing jabs at each other. "What about you, Flynn? When did you decide that Avery was your better half?"

Ryker finishes his beer and his face softens at the mention of his woman. "Avery pulled me out of the shadows," he says in a low voice. "She made me want to live again and I owe her everything."

His heartfelt words leave us both speechless for a moment. But, then Griff, as usual, has a response. "You're such a sap, Flynn. But, I'm glad."

Ryker and Griff exchange their usual handshake where they slide palms, grasp fingers and bump knuckles. At the same moment, I notice someone walking toward the pool and my pulse spikes when I realize it's Hailey. And, she's wrapped in a towel and heading to the pool where we sit.

*What the hell is she doing?*

When she drops her towel on a lounge chair and glances over at us, my gaze slides down her nearly-naked body. "Hope I'm not bothering you," she says. "I'm just going to take a quick swim."

Ryker and Griff just shrug and I narrow my eyes at her. What is she trying to prove? Parading over here in that little, two-piece suit? Giving everyone a show. I grip the arms of the chair hard, until my knuckles turn white, and watch her every lithe move.

I can't tear my gaze away as she sashays over to the edge and gracefully dives into the crystal blue water. She slices just below the surface then pops up, tilts her head back and runs her hands through her wet hair. She glances over at me and smirks.

I seriously want to yank her out of the pool, toss her over my knee and spank her.

As she swims to the opposite side of the pool, out of earshot, I realize Ryker and Griff are looking at me, trying to hold back smiles and not doing it very successfully.

"What?" I don't mean to snap, but Hailey is pissing me off.

They exchange an amused look. "She's a little young," Ryker says and I grit my jaw, "but, I can totally see it."

"For sure," Griff agrees and crosses his arms over his chest.

I frown. "See what?" I'm really annoyed and not in the mood for their teasing remarks.

"Don't even pretend that you don't have a thing for that bathing beauty."

"She's putting on quite a show for you, too," Griff adds with a smirk.

I wish he'd stop looking. I want them both to stop. "You guys are crazy," I say. "She's just a tenant."

"That makes it convenient," Griff says in a silky voice and I pierce him with a look sharper than a dagger. He holds up his hands. "Just saying."

"We are not-," *involved?* Well, we kind of are. "I don't sleep with-," *my tenants?* Well, I kind of did. "Fuck," I hiss. I run a hand through my hair and can tell that they're both smothering a laugh. "Why is this so goddamn funny?"

"Don't be so hard on yourself," Ryker says and pushes up from his chair. "Just go with it."

"Easy for you to say."

"Falling in love is never easy, buddy," Griff says and stands up. "It's pure fucking torture, but if she's worth it then you find a way to make it work. And, I promise, you'll never be happier."

I pinch the bridge of my nose and they both slap me on the back. "Good luck," Ryker says. "I need to get home and take over baby duty so Avery can sleep."

"And, I need to go rub Lexi's poor feet."

"You two are whipped," I say.

"That's love," Griff says with a shrug. Ryker just smiles and they turn and head down to the Expedition and Challenger parked at the curb.

My attention turns back to Hailey who swims around the pool like some damn mermaid. I'm about ready to drag her out and give her the tongue lashing of a lifetime. I'm not sure what kind of game she's playing, but it's pissing me off.

I jerk up out of the chair and head to the edge of the pool. When she looks over at me, all innocent, I cross my arms. "Get out," I snap. I'm still annoyed about the other night and in the mood to fight. For God's sake, I was practically celibate for over a year and the first woman I try to talk to online, Hailey sees and gets pissed off. I mean, c'mon, I'm not allowed to try to meet women like everyone else?

For fuck's sake, I'm not going to feel guilty about it. Hailey and I agreed on one time. We aren't in any kind of a serious relationship and I don't owe her anything. I fulfilled my end of the bargain and now we're supposed to go our separate ways.

So, why do we keep stalling and torturing each other?

"I wasn't aware that I was violating pool hours," she says and swims closer.

I watch her tread water in the deep end and motion to the stairs. "Out," I order between gritted teeth.

But, she doesn't listen and instead just keeps floating there, eyeing me defiantly. "No," she says.

"Hailey, I swear to God, I will come in there and get you."

Her brown eyes flash with insolence and when she doesn't budge, something in me snaps. I step off the edge and land in the water with a splash. When I swim toward her, Hailey gives a yelp and takes off toward the steps.

She may be a good swimmer, but I'm better and faster. I grab her ankle and drag her back. Hailey twists and tries to break free, but she's no match and I'm much stronger. I let go of her leg, grab her shoulders and give her a shake. "What the fuck is wrong with you? What are you trying to prove?"

"Are you crazy? Let me go!"

"No! Not until you tell me why you felt the need to parade your ass out here and show off that fucking little bathing suit?" I squeeze her upper arm. "You wanted them to notice you? To kiss you and touch you?" I know I should stop, but I can't. I'm livid. "You looking for a new fuck buddy now that you're done with me?"

Hailey's hand hits my cheek hard and my face whips to the side. Hurt fills her big, brown eyes and then it's quickly replaced by anger. "You're an asshole," she says and moves around me, heading toward the stairs.

*Fuck.* "Hailey, wait!" I turn around and follow her.

"Leave me alone!" she yells and grabs the railing to pull herself out. She hurries up the steps and grabs her towel, wrapping it around herself.

I follow her up the steps, water sluicing off my shirt and jeans, and block her from starting up the pathway to her apartment. "I said, wait, dammit!" When I reach for her arm again, she yanks it away and I see tears fill her eyes. *Oh, shit.*

"No!" She jabs a finger against my chest and pushes me back a step. "I thought you were different," she says on a sob. "But, you're worse because I trusted you. I thought you were kind and gentle and-" her voice breaks. Then, she steps around me and races to her apartment.

"Fucking...fuck!" I yell and kick a lounge chair. It takes a second to register, but I suddenly realize that half the goddamn complex is standing outside their door and watching us.

I spin around, shoving my hands through my dripping hair. Water rolls down my soaked clothes and pools down around my feet and I feel like the world's biggest jerk. *Just brilliant, Fox. Now everyone knows.*

Defeat slides through me and my head drops between my shoulders as I walk over to my corner unit. I don't know if it was a combination of sexual frustration and anger or what, but the way I lost my shit out there was completely uncalled for and not like me at all.

I walk down to the bathroom, pull my dripping clothes off and step into the shower, wishing like hell that I had managed to hang onto some semblance of control out there. But, nope. Maybe after hearing how great Ryker and Griff's lives were, I let my jealousy get the better of me.

Or, maybe Hailey Lane just has the power to drive me insane.

Either way, I know I owe her an apology. But, it's probably best if I let things cool off for a while first. The last thing I want is for the other tenants to get front row seats to another yelling match between us.

# Chapter Thirteen: Hailey

After a shower, I curl up in my bed, pull the covers up around me and cry. I'm so confused and fed up with the push and pull between Ryan and I. It's exhausting and I decide that I'm done playing games with him. If he wants to date someone he met online then fine. If he thinks I'm too young, inexperienced and not good enough for him then I guess I'll just have to accept it.

All I know is I can't keep going back to him and pretend that I'm not falling for him. Maybe if I stay away, things will get easier. *Out of sight, out of mind, right?*

The problem is I can't stop thinking about him or the hot encounters we've had. I want to be with him, but it's clear that he'd rather be with anyone but me. Like Daphne.

I need to stop obsessing over him and just let it go. That's the healthiest thing to do so that's what I vow to do from this moment forward. I am officially done with Ryan Fox, I think, and ignore the pain that constricts my heart.

When my phone beeps, I grab it and see a text from Jasmine: *Are you okay?*

*No. Not even close.* I think half the complex heard us yelling at each other and I'm so embarrassed. I type a reply and hit send: *I feel like an idiot.*

A moment later, she responds: *If it makes you feel any better, he couldn't keep his eyes off you. I think you pushed Foxy Flyboy over the edge lol...I've never seen him lose his cool or jump into the pool fully clothed.*

A half-laugh erupts from my throat. It was kind of crazy that he jumped in after me so I must've gotten under his skin.

*Don't forget,* she texts, *girls' night out tomorrow. I'm buying you a shot.*

A night out with my new friends is just what I need. I plan to dance the night away and drink myself silly. Or, at least until Ryan is a faded memory. *Can't wait,* I tell her and add a little smile emoji. I text Isa and invite her, too. I'm sure no one will mind.

The next morning, I wake up sweating and check the weather on my phone. *Ugh.* It's going to hit 100 today. I drag myself out of bed and figure I should start the air conditioner early so my place stays cool.

The window unit in the living room is small, but I'm hoping it will be powerful enough to keep the whole apartment cool. I haven't used it yet so I guess we shall see. I turn it on and frown when it makes a weird, grumbling noise. *Uh-oh.* That can't be good. But, then, it kicks on and cool air begins to pour out of the vent. *Thank God.*

I don't want to go out today, at least not until I meet the girls tonight, because it's too damn hot and I'm still humiliated that people saw Ryan and I fighting last night. Hopefully some other scandal at Sunset Terrace will surface soon and they can focus on that instead.

Wishful thinking, I know.

I spend the day choosing the set that I'm going to sing at the Magnolia Club and then practice each song over and over. I like to lay down with my headphones on sometimes and just hang off the side of my bed and sing upside down like a damn bat. It's probably silly, but it's tradition, and I just shut my eyes and feel the music. After I listen to just the music a few times through then I sing the lyrics along with it.

When I'm singing, I can normally block everything else out. But, Ryan hovers at the edge of my mind, distracting me. I try to push thoughts of him away, but it's hard. That man is such a pain in my ass. And, my heart.

Knowing what I do now, I wonder if I still would've propositioned him. Yes, I realize, no doubt about it. I don't regret it at all. Despite his tantrum last night, Ryan was patient, slow and gentle and, damn him, that's why I want more. Maybe if he would've been a little more selfish and rougher, I'd be all set.

But, no. That's not him. He took my feelings and innocence into consideration, putting my wants and needs above his own. I let out a soft sigh, pull my headphones off, and realize it's getting late. I need to eat a little something and start getting ready.

I wander out of my room and, as I head down to the kitchen, I wipe a hand across my brow. It's so stuffy here. A dip in the pool would feel great, but I can hear people out there splashing and frolicking so I'm staying in here. I can't face anyone yet.

I pull a frozen macaroni and cheese out and heat it up in the microwave. I plan to get stumbling drunk tonight so I need to make sure I have some food in my stomach to soak up all the mind-numbing alcohol I'm going to consume.

A few minutes later, I sit down with my sad little dinner and pour ketchup all over it. I love dousing my mac and cheese in ketchup and I don't care what anyone says. It's delish. While eating, I text Jasmine and ask who all is going tonight and what time I should come over. She tells me to swing by at 9pm for a pre-drink and then we will head over with Savannah and Morgan. Isa is coming straight from work and will meet us there.

I'm glad Morgan is coming. She seems cool and I hope to get to know her better. Actually, Isa, too. I know Taylor will be working, but hopefully she'll get to come over and hang with us for a bit. This will be my first experience going out since I moved to Los Angeles, so it'll be interesting. It should be fun and I'm really looking forward to it. God knows, rural Indiana didn't have any kind of nightlife.

I don't have much to wear when it comes to club clothes so I decide to wear a short, little black dress and some strappy heels. I straighten my brown hair which makes the caramel highlights pop and take my time applying my makeup. I wear it darker than usual and add some fine glitter to my eyelids to make them sparkle. Then, I slide a red-tinted gloss over my lips and spritz myself all over with my vanilla perfume. I step back and take a look at myself in the mirror. I haven't gotten this dolled up in a long time and I deserve this night out.

I grab my wristlet and head next door. When I knock, my gaze flicks over to Ryan's where a light glows in his window. He's probably chatting online with Daphne, I think with a prick of annoyance. *Whatever.* That is the last thought I plan to waste on Ryan Fox tonight, I think, as Jasmine throws the door open and pulls me inside.

"Indiana!" she cries and gives me a hug. I think she's already been drinking and I can't help but laugh.

"Are you drunk?" I ask.

"On my way," she announces and motions for me to follow her into the kitchen. "Just finished blending a pitcher of strawberry daiquiris and Morgan is on her way over now. Poor thing worked a double today and tried to bail, but I wouldn't let her."

"Sounds like we could all use a night out," I say as Jasmine pours me a glass of the frozen drink.

"Hell, yeah," she agrees. "You look gorgeous, by the way. Love the straight hair."

"Thanks," I say and check out her tiny silver skirt and beaded top. I'm sure whatever she's wearing is by a top designer and must cost a small fortune. "You look like you just stepped off the runway."

"I did!" she says and we both laugh.

As we take a sip, the door swings open and Morgan steps inside. "Hi, girls," she says and walks into the kitchen. "Ooh, yum," she says as she accepts a strawberry daiquiri from Jasmine. "This is much-needed after the day I've had."

"You work way too much, M," Jasmine says.

"I know." Her face darkens. "But, I have to." She glances at me. "My Mom is sick and her care is expensive. But, I don't want to talk about that tonight."

"No, tonight we are having fun," Jasmine announces.

"Where's Savannah?" Morgan asks.

"Home feeling like shit. She said she's sorry she can't make it, but the twins are keeping her nauseous and she's not up for dancing."

"I certainly don't blame her," Morgan says. "I can't believe she's going to have twins."

"I know, it's crazy!"

"Don't forget Isa is meeting us there," I say.

"The more, the merrier," Jazz says.

After we finish the pitcher, the girls and I take an Uber over to Club Noir. The place is packed and there's a line snaking down the sidewalk and around the corner. Jasmine glides to the front door and Morgan and I follow. She motions to the bouncer and tells him we're on the VIP list. He looks for our names and then smiles.

"Oh, you're friends with Taylor," he says and pulls out a few wristbands. He secures them around our wrists and then lifts the velvet rope. "She'll be looking for you. Have a good night, ladies." When we walk into the dark club, I have to say I feel pretty special. I've never gotten any kind of VIP treatment before.

Hip-hop music pounds and a smoke machine kicks on giving the place a misty, otherworldly quality. We head over to the bar and flash our special wristbands. "Drinks on Taylor," Jasmine says and we all laugh. The bartender whips our drinks up fast and I take a sip of my vodka sour. *Mmm.* It tastes like spiked lemonade.

"Anyone see Taylor?" Morgan asks. Her dark hair hangs down her back in waves and, in combination with her bright blue eyes, she's really striking. She wears black, faux leather leggings and a metallic shirt that slips off a shoulder. There's something very alluring, yet extremely mysterious about her.

"Over there!" Jazz points to a cage on the side of the stage where Taylor dances.

Wow, I wouldn't have recognized her. I'm used to seeing her after ballet with her hair pulled back in a tight bun and wearing a leotard. But, this Taylor is completely different. And, she has the moves.

Taylor's long red hair seems to shimmer in the flashing lights and she tosses it around as she moves to the hip-hop music thumping through the speaker. She wears a pair of fishnet stockings with tiny, torn-up denim shorts, a half shirt and military-looking black boots.

We make our way up to the cage and jump up and down, motioning to her and calling her name like fans at a rock concert. When she sees us, she drops down and a huge grin lights up her face. "You're here!" she yells above the music. "Hang on, I'm coming down."

Taylor motions for another dancer to take her place in the cage and then she hurries down the stage stairs. "Yay!" she yells and launches into us. "I'm so happy you guys are here!"

We all squeal and she guides us over to a roped-off table with a placard that reads VIP. "This is your table," she tells us and then drags a chair out and plops down. Her face glistens with sweat and she's probably been dancing for hours.

"This is great!" Jasmine says and we all sit down. It's a little quieter away from the pounding speakers and we can hear each other over the music which is nice.

"I've never been here," Morgan says.

"I know!" Taylor says. "I've been trying to get you to come down forever. Where's Savvy?"

"She called and said her morning sickness lasted til 8pm tonight. Poor thing sounded terrible."

"Aww, that's too bad," Taylor says and twists the cap off a water bottle. She gulps it down.

"Your makeup looks so cool," I say, eyeing the smoky look, and Taylor smiles.

"Thanks. I don't wear any when you usually see me after ballet."

"I know! I almost didn't recognize you up there."

Taylor looks down at her rockstar outfit and shrugs. "Not quite the same as my tutu," she says with a chuckle. She glances around the table then looks at me. "So, did I miss the conversation about you and Foxy Flyboy having it out at the pool last night?"

"Oh, God," I say and cover my face with a hand.

"Yeah, what happened?" Morgan asks. "Cody told me Ryan was yelling at you and jumped into the pool with his clothes on."

"And, that's not typical Ryan," Taylor adds. "He's always so relaxed and easygoing."

I look from Taylor to Jasmine who already knows that I slept with Ryan. Morgan doesn't know yet, but she's not stupid. "We slept together," I tell Morgan and her blue eyes widen. "It was just the one time, but…"

"But, they both want more," Jasmine says. "And, neither can fully admit it."

"Oh, geez," Morgan says.

"It's a mess," I admit.

"Do you like him?" Morgan asks.

"So much," I say and swirl the straw around the cherry in my drink. "But, now he's talking to some chippy online-"

"Daphne," Jasmine supplies.

"Daphne," I confirm, "and, I don't know what to do. This afternoon, I told myself it was over and that I was going to forget all about him. But, easier said than done."

"Men suck," Morgan says and we all laugh.

"It's much easier being single," Taylor adds.

"But, not half as fun," Jasmine says.

I let out a long sigh. "I need advice, girls."

"My advice is to forget about him and just have fun tonight," Taylor says. "Drink, dance and be merry!"

I know she's right and I nod my head. A server walks over and we all order round two. I don't want to think too hard about Ryan for the rest of the night. In fact, I'm going to banish him from my thoughts completely.

I look up and see Isa making her way over to our table. "Isa!" I jump up and wave. She looks gorgeous with her platinum blonde hair in a slick ponytail and a cute little club dress. When she gets to the table, I introduce her to Jasmine, Morgan and Taylor.

After our drinks come, Taylor tells us she has to get back to work. To help me start forgetting Foxy Flyboy, I down my drink. Jasmine and Taylor burst out laughing at how fast I suck it down and I order another one.

"Rough day?" Isa asks.

"Rough year," I say and roll my eyes.

A minute later, we decide to go down on the crowded dance floor.

The club is hot and dancers are shoulder-to-shoulder. We push past people until we get close to the center and then start dancing. I throw my head back and let my body move to the music. I haven't felt this free in a long time. All of my inhibitions melt away and I dance with my friends, letting the music take over.

I don't want to think about my uncle or Indiana or Ryan.

A few times, guys move up behind us and try to dance with us, but we ignore them. This is a girls' night and they aren't allowed to intrude into our little bubble. After dancing for almost an hour, we make our way back to the VIP table and drop down, exhausted. The server brings us another round and I blink as the room tilts.

I am drunk, I realize, and I don't even care.

I think we all are, actually. I burst out laughing, feeling really good for the first time in a long time. Jasmine, Morgan and Isa start laughing, too.

"Why are we laughing?" Morgan asks, trying to catch her breath. "Did I miss something?"

That makes me laugh even harder and suddenly we double over in a fit of giggles and no one even knows why.

Sometimes, that kind of laughter is the best of all.

# Chapter Fourteen: Ryan

I toss and turn, so damn uncomfortable and unable to sleep. It's still hot out and, even though I'm running the air conditioner, the air is heavy and has that suffocating feel to it. The only good thing that happened today is Bella texted me. We're meeting for lunch tomorrow and that gives me something to look forward to.

With a sigh, I pick up my phone and see that it's 2am.

So, I'm taken by complete surprise when a text pops up from Hailey. I slide it open: *My air conditioner is broken.*

And, she's telling me this now? At two in the morning?

It buzzes again with the red-faced emoji with its tongue hanging out.

I sit up and wonder what to do. Wait until morning to respond like a normal person who would be sleeping right now and not see this message? Or, text her back and see what she wants to do?

It is Southern California in August and I'm laying here sweating with an air conditioner that works. *Poor thing.* She must be dying over there. I text her back: *I can take a look at it.*

*When?* she asks.

*Now?* I ask.

*Okay,* she writes back.

I slide out of bed, throw my jeans on and head over. I mean, I don't want the poor girl to suffer from heat stroke. That's what I tell myself, anyway, as I lightly rap on her door. When Hailey opens it a few seconds later, I swallow hard. She's all dressed-up in a little black dress, heels and full makeup.

I raise a brow. "Did you go out tonight?" I'm glad she's out having fun while I'm here thinking about her and feeling miserable about what happened between us.

"Sure did," she says. She does a little twirl and then holds her arms out to steady herself. "That probably wasn't a good idea."

I cock my head and realize that she's drunk. Or, at least very tipsy. And, also that her apartment is hot as hell. I rub my chest and walk over to the air conditioning unit in the window. It's not even that old so I'm not sure why it would be having problems already.

Hailey moves up behind me and smells like a cone of vanilla ice cream and all I want to do is take a big bite. I grit my teeth, pull the front grille off the air conditioner and check out the air filter. Damn, it's filthy. I lift it out.

"That's disgusting," she says.

"Yeah." I go into the kitchen and run the filter under the faucet. "If the filter is dirty or clogged, it can cause all sorts of problems."

Hailey leans a hip on the counter and watches me. "Ryan?"

At the sound of her low voice, I look over and feel something warm move through me. She's looking up at me with those big, brown eyes and her face shimmers with sparkles.

"I'm sorry about the other day. I shouldn't have pushed you. You've been nothing but nice to me." She lets out a sigh and turns away. "I just have to deal with it," she adds under her breath.

"Deal with what?"

"You not wanting me." She pushes away from the counter and walks away.

My mouth drops open. *Is she kidding me?* I want her so badly that it's driving me crazy. I shake the water off the filter, wipe it with a paper towel and tell myself to put it back in the unit and leave.

*She's been drinking,* I remind myself. She doesn't know what she's saying. But, then I conveniently remember that saying about a drunk man's words are a sober man's thoughts. I set the filter down and turn around. "You really think I don't want you?"

Hailey turns, a surprised look on her face. "I-"

But, I don't give her time to respond, just take a few long strides up to her and cup her face in my hands. "Fuck, Hailey. You're *all* I think about." My gaze locks with hers and when she innocently runs that tongue across her bottom lip, I'm done. I slant my mouth down and slam it against hers.

I'm starving for her and I can't get enough. She tastes like a sweet tart and I groan into her mouth when she melts into my bare chest, kissing me back with every ounce of her being. I'm so damn tired of fighting my desire for her. I scoop her up in my arms and head back to her bedroom.

I drop her on the flower-covered comforter and look down at her, panting hard, wanting her more than I've ever wanted a woman in my life. I feel the need to mark her, make her mine, and I drop down, grab her thighs and push them apart.

Her chest rises and falls hard as she watches me. "I thought you were mad at me," she says.

"I was. You have no idea how close I was to spanking your ass for pulling that stunt at the pool."

Heat flares in her eyes and I slide my hands up under her skirt, hook my fingers in the elastic of her panties and yank them down. Unlike our first time together, I'm not feeling especially patient. But, I am feeling very, very hungry. "I'm starving for you, baby," I tell her and then dip my head under the skirt.

Hailey cries out and her hips buck up when I find her hot center and kiss her there. I want her writhing so I use my tongue, lips and teeth until she's making these little, breathy noises. I'm giving her just enough to keep here in a state of excitement, but not enough to push her over the edge. Not yet, anyway. I want to punish her first for that little show of hers the other day when Ryker and Griff were here.

"Ryan," she moans and twists.

I grab her hips and hold her so she can't move. Then, I continue to lap up her folds.

"God, please…"

"Please, what?" I ask and swirl my tongue around her clit.

"Yes, Ryan. Like that," she begs.

She's definitely begging, no doubt about it, but I let her squirm a little longer before I suck that throbbing bud into my mouth. Her whole body jerks and I can feel trembles rack her body as she cries out, coming hard.

I pull my head out from under the dress, sit back on my haunches and lick my lips. I'll never get tired of her taste. I love it. When Hailey's eyes finally flutter open, she stares up at me and I know she must see how much I want her. The raw desire rages through me and I stand up, hovering over her and ready to pounce. I want to take her now, claim her completely as I sink into her tight, little body.

But, I don't have any damn protection.

"I have to go get a condom," I rasp.

She props herself up on her elbows. "Top drawer," she says and nods to the nightstand.

"You were expecting company?" I ask, eyes narrowing.

"Just you."

With a satisfied growl, I open the drawer and pull the still-sealed box out. *My sweet girl.* I tear it open, grab a foil packet and feel her fingers drop down the back of my jeans, warm on my skin. I hiss in a breath as she slides them around and dips down further into my boxers. *Fuck.* Her fingers brush over my painfully hard cock, light and teasing. I look down and watch, letting her play and explore until I can't take it any longer.

I spin around, reach down and pull the dress over her head. For a brief moment, I admire her in the delicate lace bra, but I want her completely naked. I unsnap it and toss it aside. Her hands reach out and drag my zipper down and it's too slow, more than I can bear. With a shaky hand, I brush her fingers aside, shove my jeans and boxers down and then step forward, pushing Hailey back onto the bed, covering her with my body. I feel like I'm on fire and the feel of her satin skin against mine is like someone throwing gasoline on the flames.

I kiss her hard then pull back and rip the packet open. I need her, but not like before. This time it's different. Something feral inside me takes over and I pull her delicate frame up into my arms. Then, I turn her around, move her hair aside and begin kissing the side of her neck. I lick up to her ear and nip. "I'm going to take you like this," I tell her and push up against her backside. Hailey just moans in answer and my control snaps. I let her drop forward, lift her ass up and push, sinking my cock in her from behind.

Hailey's head whips back and a cry erupts from her mouth. I can't hold back and I thrust deeper, watching as her body stretches to take me further. "Take it, Hailey. Take it all," I say in a hoarse voice. God, she feels like heaven and I love watching her expand around me.

"Oh, God, Ryan," she moans and pushes back against me.

I reach down and around, stroking between her legs with one hand while my other holds her hips, fingers digging into the skin there. I try to keep a steady rhythm, but I'm losing control fast. I slam hard into her and begin a pounding tempo. The pressure at the base of my spine builds and, in the back of my mind, I hope I'm not hurting her. But, I don't slow down or ease up.

Suddenly, the intense, overwhelming feelings burst and I explode hard. Harder than ever before. Shudders rack through my body and I drop over her back and roar through my release. It's so fucking powerful that the edges of my vision cloud over in fuzzy blackness. "Goddammit," I swear.

The sheer, fucking intensity of it leaves my body spent. And, my heart terrified. I roll off Hailey and she drops to the mattress with a soft huff. Without a backward glance, I pad down to the bathroom, take care of the condom and still feel the aftershocks pulsing through my body. I study my face in the mirror for a minute then rub my palm against the scruff on my lower face.

In all honesty, I'm not sure what just happened. One minute, I wanted to punish her for the other day and the next, I felt like the tables turned. That I was the one who was at her mercy instead. And, I'm not sure how I feel about that.

The tides are shifting and it's becoming more and more clear that I'm the one who needs her now. And, not the other way around. I slide my hand around to the back of my neck and squeeze. *This isn't good*. All of a sudden, I just want to get out of here. To bolt and erase Hailey Lane from my mind once and for all.

Once my breathing gets under control, I cross the hall and warily step back into her room. God, it's hot and it smells musky like sex and fucking. Christ, I can feel myself starting to get hard again.

Hailey lays against the pile of pillows, sheet pulled up and, thankfully, covering her. I don't know what to say after that so I just reach down and tug my jeans on, keeping my gaze averted.

"Ryan?"

I pull the zipper up, but leave the button undone. "Hmm?" Even though I don't want to, I finally look over at her. God, I feel like I'm under some kind of spell. Like she's bewitched me. Because all I want to do is fuck her again.

"Are you okay?"

*No. You're turning me inside out, little girl.* "Sure," I mumble. I glance over at the door and just want to get the hell out of here.

"I liked it that way," she says, voice low and sultry.

My eyes slide shut. I give a sharp nod, but my nostrils flare and my cock surges to life.

"Please, stay," she says.

"I can't," I force out between gritted teeth.

Suddenly, she gets up and walks over to me. Her hand dips and covers the front of my jeans. "Will you show me other ways?"

"Jesus, Hailey." She's killing me.

"You're hard." Down the zipper goes and my cock springs free.

*Dammit.*

Her fingers wrap around me. "Hard like steel, but silky like satin."

"Hailey, please…"

"Please, what?" she asks, echoing my words from earlier.

I finally look at her and those brown eyes of hers glow. *Please, understand that we can't keep doing this.*

"Show me what to do, Ryan." Her fingers brush lightly up and down and I know I'm not going anywhere.

I wrap my hand around hers and start pumping hard and fast. If she wants a lesson then I'll give her one. I'll give her one she'll never forget. I guide her finger over the head of my cock and rub it there until it's wet with moisture.

"I want to put my mouth on you. Like you do to me." Then, without warning, Hailey drops to her knees and my pulse spikes.

*God. In. Heaven.* When her lips wrap around me, I think I grow another inch. Hailey sucks me into her mouth, cheeks indenting, and my hips jerk forward. "Holy hell, Hailey," I gasp, fingers threading into her hair. Even though she's doing pretty well on her own, I guide her head and set the pace. Then, I lose all train of rational thought and let her have at it.

Game over. I'm done. I've come to accept that this little girl will be the death of me.

I can feel my release coming fast and I know I should warn her, but my mind is barely functioning at this point. It's all too much and I come hard and ground out a long, rumbling, "*Fuuuck.*"

I pull Hailey up into my arms and kiss her hard. Then, I bury my face into her fragrant hair and sigh. I have no idea what to do about her anymore. If I run, she finds me. When I push her away, she lures me back.

"Will you stay with me?" she asks.

I feel the last of my defenses crumble away and I cup her face. "Yeah," I say, finally giving in to her. To us. "I'll stay."

The next morning after I sneak back to my place, I can't stop thinking about our night together. *Fucking heaven.* Everything about it was perfect. Because Hailey is perfect. I lost count of how many times we did it after I agreed to stay the night.

Needless to say, I'm exhausted, completely worn out and totally satiated like I've never been before. I finish my coffee and then take a long shower imagining what we could do in here under the pounding water. And, I can imagine quite a bit.

This time, before I go over to meet Bella, I text her to make sure she remembers. She promises to be there at noon so I head over to the vegan restaurant with her belated birthday gift. It's not as crowded today and I wait out on the same bench. She's only five minutes late today and, when I see her walk up, I stand and give her a hug.

"Happy Birthday, Bella-Vanilla," I say and hand her the present.

"Ugh, don't call me that. And, you didn't have to get me anything," she says. "But, thank you." I may be prejudiced, but I think Bella is beautiful. She ended up getting the best traits from Paige and I-- my light green eyes and Paige's pale blonde hair. She resembles a fairy or angel with her petite frame. But, looks can be deceiving because my daughter has a fiery side and, unfortunately, it's burned me a few times.

We sit down at a table on the patio and I nod to the gift. "Open it," I tell her.

"I'd rather wait," she says. But, I think she must see the disappointment flash across my face because then she changes her mind. "Oh, alright." Bella tears the paper off and eyes the chess set.

"Remember when you told me how much you liked to play?"

"Yeah, when I was like 10." She laughs.

I frown. "No, it was just a couple years ago."

Bella sets it on the chair next to her. "Thanks, Dad."

"There's another box," I say, feeling a little deflated.

"Oh, right." Bella opens it and lifts the necklace up. "It's pretty. Thanks."

I get the feeling that she doesn't really like it. "You hate it," I say.

She looks up at me and shrugs. "I'm sorry. It's just that I don't ever wear gold." She lifts her hands to show me the silver rings and bracelets.

I feel like an idiot. "I can take it back and exchange it."

"It's fine," she says and sets the box on the chess set.

I stifle a sigh. "So, how have you been?" I ask.

She seems to light up a bit. "Good. I'm making a lot of tips at work and I've been seeing this new guy who I really like."

"That's great. How's school?"

"Classes are classes. But, I'm almost done so it's good."

"If you need any help with your tuition-"

"I got it covered."

I hate how she never wants to accept anything from me. How she keeps me at arm's length. The waiter brings our food and she dives into the mushy-looking soup and tofu burger with zeal. At least I got the restaurant right.

I take a bite of my fajita wrap filled with grilled soy chicken and try not to make a face. *Blech.* I don't know how she can be a vegan, but I'm proud of her. I swallow down the cardboard-tasting food and know that I couldn't ever do it.

"Dad?"

I look up from picking some slimy shit out of the wrap. "Huh?"

"You know Mom is dating someone, right?"

Actually, I had no idea. "No, I didn't know. But, I'm happy for her."

Bella's eyes narrow.

God, they look so much like my eyes, I realize. "What?"

"You're happy for her? Really?"

I hear the disbelief in her voice and set my fork down. "Why wouldn't I be?"

"Well, I didn't think you ever really cared about her feelings. Or, mine, for that matter."

"Isabella, that is not true." How could she think that I didn't care?

"Could've fooled me."

Her tone cuts me to the quick. "Look, I'm not sure what your mother has told you about the divorce, but I'm assuming the blame was all placed on me because I worked so much."

"Do you deny that?"

"No, but you have to understand how young we were when we got married. Neither of us was ready, but she was pregnant and we wanted to try to make things work. Honestly, honey, I think our relationship was over before we even said our vows."

Bella gives me a funny look. "How old were you?"

"I was 20 and Paige was 19." I can see the gears turning in her head and wonder if she didn't know this.

"I guess I thought you were older," she murmured. "So, you weren't already in the military?"

I shake my head. "No. Not until a few years later."

"So, you guys were together then. For at least a few years before you started flying."

"Yeah. I worked at a grocery store and she was home with you. It was hard making ends meet. Nobody went through diapers like you, kid."

"Dad!" She bursts out laughing and it's like music to my ears.

"I knew I had to find a better job so I could support you both and I had a friend in the Army and he made it sound like a pretty good deal. So, I joined and found out I had a talent for flying."

"And, then you just flew away."

"No. You and your Mom came with me and we lived on the base in Fort Campbell, Kentucky, while I trained."

"We lived in Kentucky?"

I nod, surprised she didn't know.

"And, then what happened?"

"I finished my training and started going out on missions. Your Mom wanted to move back here and so we did. But, we'd grown apart even more and one day we sat down and decided neither of us was happy." I meet my daughter's gaze and give her a small, sad smile. "We tried, Bella. We tried really hard for you."

Bella looks away fast and grabs her water. I'm not sure if I saw right, but it almost looked like tears brightened her eyes. For a split second, anyway.

She swallows down a few sips and seems to be mulling over what I just told her. "I didn't know a lot of that," she says. "Thank you for telling me."

I reach over and wrap my hand around hers. "You're welcome." And, for the first time since I can remember, Bella gives me a genuine smile and it feels really, really good. "Love you, Bella-Vanilla," I say and squeeze her hand.

She doesn't say it back, but she does give my hand a squeeze.

*I'll take it,* I think, feeling like we made a bit of a breakthrough today. I'm so happy that I take a big bite of the slimy soy wrap.

# Chapter Fifteen: Hailey

After my mind-blowing night with Ryan, I couldn't be happier. If my smile was any wider, I think my lips would split. Things are going really well and that's unusual for me so I can't help but wonder when something bad will happen.

I try to stay positive, though, and be grateful that Ryan seems to have come around. Whatever was holding him back before sure didn't last night, I think, unable to ignore the soreness between my legs. He had been positively ravenous and insatiable. Normally, so controlled, I'd never seen that side of him before. The man is sexy as hell and, I'm not going to lie, I liked it. A lot.

My big gig at the Magnolia Club is coming up fast and I am so excited. I've been inviting everyone to go and I hope they can come out so there will be some friendly faces in the audience. So far, I know Jasmine and Taylor will be there for sure. Oh, and I texted Isa and she said she's coming, too.

And, last night, I asked Ryan if he was coming. He said he wouldn't miss it for the world.

Yeah, things are definitely going well.

I should've known that my luck wouldn't hold out and everything would turn to shit by tonight.

I plan to practice my set all day, work on different improv and singing techniques and drink lots of water. As a singer, my vocal cords are my instrument and I need to keep them healthy so I can exercise my full range.

It's vital that I always warm up my voice before singing and I run through plenty of exercises that probably look super silly. But, I don't care. I spend at least 20 minutes warming up my facial muscles and loosening my lips and jaw muscles by blowing through my lips, sticking out my tongue and massaging my face.

I let my voice wander up and down its range then move on to humming and then some gentle lip rolls and tongue trills. Once my face, mouth and voice feel loose, I allow myself to start singing. Some people sing from their throat, but any true singer knows that the real power behind your voice is your breath. And, your breath should be supported by your diaphragm. Singing from my core allows my vocal cords to relax and lets my voice resonate in my chest, pharynx and face.

I practice for hours, hydrate nonstop and then decide to take a break. I hear some voices from outside and glance out the window to see Cody and Mason splashing around in the pool. As fun as they are, I'd rather sneak over to Ryan's place.

But, I'm reluctant. Even though we had the most amazing night, a part of me is still nervous that I could scare him away. It might be safer to start with a text and see how he responds. *Hmm.* As I debate what to do, my phone dings with a text from him: *Hi, sweetheart. Just wanted to say last night was incredible. I'm meeting my daughter for lunch, but let's talk when I get back.*

It was beyond incredible, I think. His text gives me the boost of confidence that I need and I write back: *See you then, Foxy Flyboy…*

I know my response will make him laugh and I'm glad he wants to talk. I'm done pretending that there's nothing between us and I hope he feels the same way. Because there's no denying the pull and the chemistry. When we come together, something electric happens. And, I know how rare that is-- for me, anyway. I've truly never felt anything like it before on this kind of heart and soul level.

Ryan was married before which means he was in love before. I wonder how his ex-wife differs from what we have together? Did he have this kind of hot, vibrant, all-consuming need for her like he does for me? Like I have for him? I want to have these conversations with him. I want to get to know him better.

I feel like I'm standing at the top of a very steep slope and I still have the choice of stepping back before I get sucked down the side of the mountain. As much as I'm starting to care for Ryan, I know if things ended now, I'd be in a much better position than if they ended three months from now.

*Oh, who am I kidding?* I gave the man my virginity-- well, I kind of forced it on him-- and now I've developed all sorts of feelings for him. Really strong feelings that make me want to throw my arms around him and see where the road leads us. I can't help it. I've always been a bit impulsive and tend to act on instinct rather than think things through.

And, right now, my instinct is telling me that Ryan is the one.

Now, I just need him to see what I see.

A few hours later, there's a knock on my door and my heart begins to pound. I know it's Ryan and when I open the door, he stands there looking so very handsome in a black t-shirt, jeans, boots and a baseball cap that makes him look boyish. "Hi," he says and swoops in, pulling me up against his hard body and then capturing my mouth in a slow, hungry kiss. I wrap my arms around his neck and sigh into his mouth.

"How was your lunch?" I ask. I can feel his good mood and it makes me happy.

"Really good," he says. "For the first time in a long time, Bella and I actually talked."

"I'm glad," I tell him and drop my head back as his lips dip to my neck, leaving a trail of moist kisses.

"Do you have any plans this afternoon?" he asks and looks up, green eyes glittering.

I shake my head.

A bright, white smile lights his handsome face up and then he drops a kiss on the tip of my nose. "Good because I'm taking you on a little adventure."

"Really?" I give a little squeal.

"Yep, so throw your shoes on and let's roll."

I laugh and feel a surge of excitement fill me as I slip my shoes on and grab my purse. We head out and Ryan grabs my hand and squeezes as we walk over to his truck. I hear a hush fall over the pool area and know that Cody and Mason are watching us.

My throat constricts with emotion when I realize that Ryan is announcing to the world that we are together. This is a huge step and I can't believe it's actually happening. He wants to be with me and he values me more than just keeping our relationship some dirty, little secret.

Ryan opens the passenger side door and I hop into the truck. As he makes his way around and slides into the driver's seat, I look over and admire his gorgeous profile. When he glances over and studies me with those light green eyes, my stomach fills with butterflies.

"Where are we going?" I ask.

"You'll see," he says with a mysterious smile. We merge onto the 101 N and even though I try to get more information out of him, he's not spilling anything. "I like your hat," I say. The top part of the patch says "Special Operations Aviation Regiment" and "Death Waits In The Dark" curves along the bottom. In the center, there's a symbol that's half man, half winged-horse and he holds a blade. Above him, it reads "160th" and below it says "Night Stalkers."

"Thanks," he says, completely humble.

I'm beginning to understand that being a Night Stalker is a pretty big deal. And, definitely not an easy accomplishment or for the faint of heart. I really admire Ryan because every time he went out in the black night to fly Spec Ops soldiers on secret missions, he was risking his life for them and his country.

Ryan Fox is a damn good man. And, a complete badass.

By the time we exit at Vineland, I realize we're in Burbank and I have no idea where he's taking me.

But, I can tell he's really looking forward to it and an excited energy flows off him and it's utterly contagious. I'm getting antsy and I really just want to know what we're going to do. Then, I see the sign for the Hollywood-Burbank Airport.

"Oh, my gosh. Are we-"

"Going flying," he finishes with another big smile.

My nerves kick in and I don't want to tell him that I'm scared of flying. But, he reads me easily and when the truck rolls to a stop, he reaches over and grabs my hand.

"Are you scared?"

I give a little nod, feeling like a big baby.

"You don't like to fly? Or, you've had a bad experience?"

"I've never actually even been in a plane before," I admit.

"Never?" He tugs me closer and kisses me. "Well, we're going in a helicopter and you're going to love it," he promises.

I put on a brave face and we head over to a helicopter which waits outside a large hangar. It's so intimidating and the idea that Ryan used to fly these all the time makes me feel better. I know I'm in the best hands possible.

"Is this yours?" I ask, a little in awe.

"No, it belongs to Jax Wilder, but he's letting us borrow it." I raise a brow. "You know Ryker and Griff who were over the other night? They work for Jax who runs Platinum Security. His wife is Easton Ross and she gave him this bird as an engagement gift."

"Easton Ross, the actress?" I ask, not quite sure I heard him right

"The one and only."

"Oh, I love her!"

"Maybe you can meet her sometime," he teases.

"Oh, my gosh, I wouldn't even know what to say."

"You have nothing to worry about. She's very nice."

"You've met her?"

"Sure."

He sounds so nonchalant, like he doesn't even care that she's one of the biggest stars in the world. It's one of the things I love about him. Always so calm and cool. I can see how he would've made an amazing pilot.

And, I guess I'm about to find out as he tells me we'll leave after he finishes his pre-check. I watch him walk around the helicopter, checking various things thoroughly. This is obviously not his first rodeo and I'm impressed that he knows this machine like the back of his hand. He talks to another man there, the mechanic, I think, and I have no idea what they're saying. I do not understand "pilot speak" and it's like they're talking in another language.

Then, he motions for me to come over. "Ready?" he asks.

I force a nod and follow him around where he helps me up. After he shows me how to buckle in and hands me a pair of noise-cancelling headphones, he taps the tip of my nose and grins. "Don't be nervous. Your real fear is of the unknown, of what could happen. But, I'm not going to let anything bad happen to you, Hailey. I'm highly-trained and have more experience than you could ever imagine."

He jumps out, walks around and gets into the pilot's seat. I can see the happiness on his face as he puts his headphones on and then talks to the tower. Above us, the rotors spin and after he receives takeoff clearance, he looks over at me and tells me I'm about to have the best experience of my life.

I don't know about that because I think that may have happened last night when he spent the night with me. Nevertheless, I try to suppress my nerves and hang on tight as I feel the helicopter begin to lift and suddenly we're airborne.

"Oh, *wow*," I say and hear him chuckle. "This is absolutely incredible." We're gliding through the sky at low-level and I'm grinning from ear-to-ear, all of my earlier trepidation gone. "It's exhilarating! Absolutely breathtaking!"

"You're breathtaking!" he says.

I watch him effortlessly work the controls and we ascend higher and higher. This is so beautiful, so inspiring. "I feel like a bird!" I say and laugh.

"You sing like one, too," he says and I smile. "It's liberating, isn't it?"

I nod and we soar toward downtown Los Angeles. Seeing the city from this perspective gives me a whole new appreciation for it. Ryan reaches over and takes my hand. He points out certain landmarks and he's the perfect tour guide. "Feel free to take pictures," he says.

Next thing I know, my camera is snapping one shot after another. And, quite a few of them are Ryan and how attractive he looks behind the controls.

After flying around DTLA for a bit, Ryan guides us west and soon we are moving over the ocean and the shoreline.

"Hailey, look," he says and points down where I spot a group of dolphins swimming through the waves.

"Oh, my gosh! Dolphins!"

I snap a ton of pictures and feel like the luckiest girl in the world. I feel so comfortable with Ryan flying and all of my earlier fear is gone.

Unfortunately, the flight has to come to an end and before I'd like, we're landing back in Burbank at the airport. Ryan smoothly lowers us onto the tarmac and I let out a long breath and sink back in the seat. What a ride!

"Well? What did you think of your first helo ride?"

"I have no words," I say. "Amazing…"

I instantly think back to our first time together at the hotel. Ryan Fox really has a way of leaving me speechless.

"Want to get something to eat?" he asks.

"I'd love to," I say.

"Do you like Mexican food?" he asks and I nod.

It's nice when the man asks and doesn't assume, I think. But, of course, Ryan would ask. He's a perfect gentleman and always puts my wants and needs first.

Ryan takes me to a popular Mexican restaurant on Ventura Boulevard and it's delicious. We order a few different dishes and feast on everything from tacos to burritos to nacho chips with fresh guacamole. He drinks a couple of Coronas with lime and I manage to drink two strawberry margaritas.

I can't remember the last time I had such a good time with a man or one who made me laugh so much. When I ask him to tell me more about his days as a Night Stalker, Ryan launches into a few different stories. I know everything he did was classified so he doesn't go into any detail, but I do see him in a different light.

The missions he used to fly give me chills. To successfully fly these highly-trained Special Operatives in pitch blackness during the middle of the night, bad weather and in and out of enemy territory had to be extremely nerve-wracking, but when I ask, Ryan just shrugs.

"It's just what I did," he says easily. "I didn't have time to be worried or nervous. My job was to get them in and out smoothly so that's what I did."

"You're a hero," I tell him.

He shakes his head. "Nah. It was just a job and I did it well. If I hadn't, I certainly wouldn't be sitting here right now."

"Don't even say that," I say, completely horrified at the idea. But, I know it's true.

I'm extremely grateful for this time with Ryan and we find ourselves chatting for a very long time. I love getting to know all of the details about him and ask a ton of questions.

"What's your middle name?"

"Justin," he says.

"Ryan Justin Fox. I really like that."

"My Grandpa's name was Justin," he says. "How about you?"

"Aurora."

He smiles. "I love that," he says. "It fits you."

I tilt my head. "Really? How so?"

"Because Aurora was the Roman goddess of the dawn who traveled from east to west announcing the coming of the sun. I guess as a pilot, I can appreciate your connection with the sky."

"You can be quite the romantic," I say.

"Me? Nah. I just like to find the deeper connection between things."

"I bet your favorite color is blue."

He nods. "You're quite perceptive. Sky blue, all the way. You?"

"I always liked yellow."

"Because you're a little songbird. Like a canary."

I laugh. "I don't know about that. Yellow just always symbolized hope to me. It's bright and makes me think of the sun. Reminds me that no matter what bad things may happen today, there's always tomorrow and hopefully better things on the horizon."

"You're the romantic."

"Maybe," I admit and finish my drink. I study him over the flickering candlelight and this time, I feel something more than mere butterflies. It's a feeling that runs deeper, more intense.

*I'm falling in love with him,* I realize. Although a little scary, the thought sits well with me because no one deserves to be loved more than Ryan Fox. And, I'm going to love him fiercely, with everything I've got.

# Chapter Sixteen: Ryan

*Today was literally the perfect day,* I think as I float on my back in the pool. I was back in the skies, doing what I love, and I was with the woman I-

I let out a long breath. Here's where things get complicated, I realize, as the word *love* floats around in my head. It's not possible that I can be in love with someone so soon after meeting her, my rational side tells me. I'm a thinker, a planner, a man who doesn't let his emotions rule his life.

Yet, the simple fact is I can't stop thinking about Hailey Aurora Lane. I know it's silly, but when she told me her middle name over dinner tonight, I wasn't surprised. It's like I knew that it would be somehow related to the skies. To the thing I love most in this world.

I want to know everything about her and we ended up spending over two hours at the restaurant getting to know each other better.

I've also decided that I want to pursue a relationship with her and I know that we may get some backlash because of our age difference, but I really don't care anymore. I've never been so happy as I am when I'm with her. At the same time, it doesn't mean I'm quite ready to announce it to the world yet, either. I like to move more slowly when it comes to anything serious with a woman.

I'm smart enough to know that we won't be able to keep it under wraps for long, though, especially at Sunset Terrace, so I purposely held her hand in front of everyone when we passed by the pool earlier today. I'm sure the news spread like wildfire, but I have a feeling most people already figured it out. Especially after our screaming match and when I jumped in the pool with my clothes on like a complete lunatic.

The sun is starting to go down and I swim over to the edge and pull myself out. Dripping water, I walk over to the nearest lounge chair, grab my towel and wipe my face and chest off. My mind wanders to tonight and I'm looking forward to spending it with Hailey.

Right now she's over at Jasmine's and I can only imagine what they're talking about. *Us,* I'm pretty sure. But, what does it matter? I'm claiming Hailey as mine and there's nothing that anyone can say or do about it.

After I take a shower, I pull on some pajama bottoms and check my phone. When I read the text from Hailey saying she'll be over at 9pm, my cock twitches. I'm not sure how we can possibly have a better time tonight than last night, but I'm willing to give it a try. I also have a message from Bella and I hit play.

I'm a little surprised it's a voicemail since she never calls. Only sends text messages.

*"Hi, Dad. I just wanted to say that I had a really nice time with you today and, I don't know, I was thinking that maybe, if you want, we can start doing weekly lunches together? To catch up or whatever. Just an idea. Anyway, sorry I missed you and talk to you soon."*

I really can't express how happy I am that she called and I immediately dial her back. And, to my surprise, she actually answers.

"Hi, Dad."

"Hey, Bella-Vanilla, I just got your message and, yes, I think that's a terrific idea-- to meet for lunch each week."

"Really? I wasn't sure if you had the time-"

"I always have time for you, honey. And, if I didn't, I'd make it." When she doesn't say anything, I let out a small sigh and press forward. "You're the most important thing in my life and I hope you know that. I want to see you more and to have you in my life. I've missed you so much and you mean the world to me and-" *Fuck*. My voice catches with emotion.

"Are you okay?" she asks.

"I've never been better," I say in complete honesty.

"Well, I'm not sure what your schedule is like, but maybe we could meet Saturdays at noon? And, we don't always have to go to a vegan place," she adds. I can hear the smile in her voice.

"That would be really great," I tell her. There's this pressure rising in my chest and I rub a hand over it, suddenly feeling ridiculously emotional over such a small thing. But, for us, this is a big step.

"Oh, just not this Saturday, okay? I already made plans to go listen to my friend sing at the Magnolia Club."

A strange tingling skitters down my spine. "The Magnolia Club?"

"Yeah, it's this jazz club over on Sunset. I met this girl and we've hung out a couple times and she's a singer. So, she invited me to her gig. Isn't that cool?"

*Oh, no.* There's a sinking feeling in the pit of my stomach and there's no way she could be talking about Hailey. The world isn't that small or cruel.

"Her name is Hailey and she just moved here from Indiana."

*Fuck.*

"Anyway, other than this Saturday, I'm good."

*Isabella and Hailey are friends? How did this even happen?*

I'm having trouble wrapping my head around it, but tell her that's fine. Inside, though, I'm reeling. Just when I thought I was ready to try things with Hailey, I realize that I don't want my daughter to know that I'm not only sleeping with someone her age, but also her friend.

*Shit, shit, shit.*

This is literally the worst-case scenario. Bella and I are finally finding some common ground and communicating and I couldn't be more thrilled. But, how is she going to react when she finds out that I'm sleeping with her friend?

What if she's pissed? Disgusted? Decides that she doesn't want to have a relationship with me after all? Is that a chance I'm willing to take?

I've worked hard to stay in Bella's life and want nothing more than to have a strong father-daughter relationship with her. But, I'm terrified that being in a romantic relationship with Hailey could potentially ruin all of that.

I think I know my daughter well enough to know that she wouldn't want a step-mother that's her age and her friend.

*God, this is fucking twisted,* I think. How could things have gone from so damn amazing to this? I feel like I'm back in the cockpit and spinning out of control. I didn't tell Hailey the story of when I crash-landed during one of my missions.

But, it wasn't the enemy fire and near RPG hit that took us down. It was a bolt of lightning. The storm had been bad, really intense, and I was flying the guys through dangerous territory. At the time of the strike, two SEALs were rappelling down beneath the Blackhawk and I'll never forget the loud, cracking sound that had filled the air.

Then, even more frightening, was the eerie silence that followed when the engine noise suddenly decreased to idle and the ground came rushing up at an alarming rate.

In my training, I learned how to autorotate a helicopter. It's something that all helicopter pilots practice. Basically, as soon as the engine loses power, the pilot lowers the collective to spin up the main rotor as the aircraft loses altitude, or at least reduce the rate at which the rotor is slowing. Then, just above the emergency landing spot, the pilot pulls up on the collective to increase the angle of attack and create more upward thrust. This slows the aircraft's rate of descent in preparation for the landing.

Right before we hit hard, the two SEALS rappelling beneath the Blackhawk released their rope, letting their snap links be the only thing slowing their descent. Then, right before impact, those fuckers jumped back inside and told me they watched as the rotors impacted the ground, broke up and went flying around the LZ.

Once we were out of enemy range and safely back at base, we all had a pretty good laugh about it and got roaring drunk. But, close calls and heart attack situations were all a part of the job. You couldn't dwell on it and the fact that we made it out safely is all that mattered.

But, for that split second when the engine first goes out on a bird, panic and fear slide through your belly like a slick, oily serpent. You know there is no guarantee that you're going to survive, but you stay calm and let the thousands of hours of training and endless experience take over.

And, hopefully, it's enough to get you through.

I run a hand over my face and look down at my phone. It's 9pm and, right on time, Hailey knocks on my door.

Right now, I have that same feeling as I did when the engine in the Blackhawk stopped and we began to plummet. But, unlike last time, I have no idea what to do. No training has prepared me for this and I can't deal with it right now.

When I open the door, Hailey breezes in looking so happy and my gut twists. She pushes up on her tiptoes to kiss me and I pull back. I see the confusion flicker through her big, brown eyes and I take a step back. "Hailey-"

"What's wrong?"

"I'm just, um, not feeling well."

Her face falls. "Oh, no. Can I get you anything? Make you some tea?"

"Thanks, but no. I think I'm just going to go to bed early."

"Oh, okay." She lays a hand over my cheek and smiles. "If you need anything, let me know. I'm sorry you're not feeling well, but I understand. And, I need you to rest up so you'll be all healthy for my gig Saturday."

Now my stomach really hurts. Just the thought of seeing Bella there and having to explain what I'm doing there, too...*Shit.* I'd rather be back in that crashing Blackhawk, hurtling toward the ground.

*What am I doing?* Suddenly, the thought hits me hard that I am being a complete coward. This is where I'm supposed to be an adult and talk things out. Even though we had the most wonderful day, I start questioning if we're moving too fast. Bella's revelation shocked me, but it also put things back into perspective.

It reminds me how I should listen to my gut which originally warned me to stay away from Hailey. She's too young, too tempting, too everything. I should turn my attention elsewhere. To someone more appropriate like Darla. I mean Daphne. *Dammit.* I can't think straight when my nostrils are full of Hailey's soft vanilla smell.

"Hailey..." She looks up at me, trusting me not to hurt her, but I don't know how this can end well. I let out a sigh and grit my jaw hard. "I know you're friends with Bella."

She frowns. "Who?"

"My daughter." She looks at me like I'm crazy.

"I don't know anyone named Bella."

"Isabella? She told me she's going to your gig Saturday."

Something clicks in her brown eyes. "Isa? Isa is your daughter?"

I didn't think she really used that nickname anymore, but apparently I was wrong. "Yeah and we're trying to mend our relationship, but I'm not sure how she would react to...us being together."

A million emotions cross her face. "I had no idea she was your daughter. But, if you're happy, isn't that all that matters?"

I shake my head. "It's not that simple. Bella blames me for a lot, especially for the divorce, and this is the first time things are starting to go well for us. I feel like I'm still walking on eggshells, though, and I don't want to do anything to upset her."

"And you think that if she found out about us that she'd be mad?"

"My biggest fear is that I would lose my daughter. For good." I reach for Hailey's hands, lift them up and place a kiss on their backs. "I don't think that's a chance I can take, Hailey."

Her face falls and I feel like the world's biggest jerk. "After everything we've done," she whispers. "And, after today…" Her voice catches and it feels like a knife just stabbed into my heart.

"I need you to understand-"

"Oh, I do. I understand that you think you have to choose between me and your daughter. And, that I'm not worth the risk." Hailey pulls her hands away and gives me the saddest look I've ever seen. "No one said you have to make a choice. You didn't even try, Ryan."

Then, she walks out. I have the urge to reach out and grab her, but I don't. Instead, I lean against the doorframe and drop my head into my arm.

One of the best days of my life just turned into the worst.

Later that night, I pull a chair up next to the window and hear Hailey singing. Her voice sounds melancholy and I know that's because of me. *Oh, my little nightingale, I'm so sorry.* Just like the little bird, she always sings at night and never tires of it.

For as long as she sings, I listen and wonder whether I made a huge mistake. But, then I think about Bella and know that a good father would put his daughter's needs and wants first. Before his own.

Even so, I know that giving up Hailey is going to be the hardest thing that I have ever done.

# Chapter Seventeen: Hailey

The rest of the week passes by so torturously slowly and I try to focus on my singing and perfecting my set for Saturday, but it's hard to concentrate when my heart is breaking. Ryan infiltrates every one of my thoughts, his final words haunting me day and night.

*I don't think that's a chance I can take, Hailey.*

Meaning, me. I am not worth him trying to have a relationship with and the thought leaves me bereft and empty. I would never expect or ask him to sacrifice his relationship with his daughter. I know how much she means to him and how important it is that they mend their relationship. But, at the same time, he's just assuming that Isabella wouldn't understand.

I've spent some time with her and I think Isa would be more understanding than he thinks. Especially since she knows me and we're friends. Maybe it would be a little weird at first, but Ryan needs to think about himself, too. He's always putting everyone else's needs before his own and, as much as I adore that about him, it's also not healthy.

No one can predict Isa's reaction. But if we sit down and talk it out like adults, she may be more accepting than not. It's a risk, of course, but Ryan needs to be honest with her. And, with himself.

But, he'd rather forget us and pretend nothing ever happened. And, so much did happen. I can't forget how much fun we had when we went flying and then out to dinner. For the first time, it felt like we were a real couple, on a date and getting to know each other. I loved hearing about his life and there's still so much more that I want to know.

We connect on every level and I think he owes it to himself, and to us, to try. To talk to Isa and explain the situation. She's an adult now, not a moody teenager, and she's falling in love herself with a man named Shawn. She gushes about him all the time.

I shake my head and sigh. If Ryan doesn't want to do it then there's nothing I can do. He needs to want me and a relationship, and I won't force him. He can be pretty stubborn, though, and once he makes up his mind about something, I have a feeling that it's going to be hard to change it.

Ryan told me that Night Stalkers don't quit. That's the motto they live by, but he quit on me.

I'm not quite sure how I'm supposed to pretend nothing ever happened between us. Each time we were together, I gave him a little piece of my heart, foolishly trusting that he would keep it safe. And, now, I have nothing left. He holds it all in his hands.

And, he's crushing it.

I swallow back a new onslaught of tears and refuse to shed anymore for a man who doesn't want me. He's not worth it, I try to convince myself.

Unfortunately, I've never been able to lie to myself.

By now, I've looked through the pictures on my phone about a thousand times from when we went flying. I have to stop. I toss my phone aside and do my best to push Ryan out of my head and focus on tonight. This performance could make or break me. If there's an agent or record producer in the audience, being able to sing in front of them is the opportunity of a lifetime. Careers have been made overnight when the right person happens to be in the right place at the right time.

On the flip side, if I screw up, word will get around fast that I am not talented and not worth anyone's time. Industry people will trash my emails and demos without even listening to them. I can't afford to have a bad reputation or my dream of singing will end before it ever begins.

I'll have to get a job at a restaurant or bar as a server because that's all I'm qualified for and, if I can't find one, then I'll run out of my savings fast. Los Angeles is very expensive and I would probably find myself living in my car, struggling to get by.

God knows, I don't want to move back to Indiana. It's the last thing I would do, but if the situation becomes desperate…

*No.* You're going to sing your ass off tonight and impress the hell out of everyone in that audience. Because that's what you do.

After I give myself a pep talk, I start to get ready for tonight. I do my makeup, put on a simple black dress and heels and then tuck a gardenia behind my ear. My hair hangs long and loose and the flower is to help me channel my inner Billie Holiday.

After I'm ready, I start my vocal exercises and then run through my set. I've been drinking water all day to keep my vocal cords moistened and when Jasmine and Taylor come over at 6pm, I'm ready.

"You look stunning!" Jasmine gushes.

"You're gonna knock 'em dead," Taylor enthuses.

"I hope so," I say and wipe my palms down my dress.

Neither of them knows what happened with Ryan and I don't plan on telling them right now. So, when Jazz asks if Ryan will meet us there, I just smile and nod. But, I have no idea if he will show up or not.

When we arrive at the Magnolia Club, I pause in the entranceway and just take it all in, absorbing the beauty and energy of the room. It's beautiful with dark red, satin-covered walls and has a speakeasy, boudoir feel. Small round tables and chairs closely surround the stage and there's an intimate feel to it.

A lot of singers have been discovered here and I hope to be one of them.

Jasmine guides us to a couple of tables right up front. I'm glad we got here a little early so I can listen to some of the other performers and also because the place fills up fast. It's not long before the gang shows up. Cody and Mason find us, give me hugs and pull up chairs. Not long after, Isa arrives and tells me how excited she is for me. I study her for a long moment and realize that she has the exact same light green eyes as Ryan. I don't know why I didn't notice it before. My chest tightens and I wonder what she would say if she knew about me and Ryan. I can't think about that right now, though. When Morgan shows, I'm so happy she made it. I know she works and visits her Mom on the weekend so it means a lot that she came out for me tonight.

As it nears 7pm, I know it's time to go backstage and get ready.

Everyone wishes me good luck and I thank them for coming. It really means the world to me.

Unfortunately, the most important person, the man I want to be here the most, isn't and I just have to accept it.

The manager of the club runs over a few reminders and the pianist who will accompany me on a few of the songs already has the sheet music. I'm ready, I think.

"Good luck," the manager says.

"Thank you," I say and then find myself all alone, waiting for the singer before me to finish his set. After he's done, there's a smattering of applause and he walks past me, not looking happy with his performance.

"Good job," I tell him and he nods at me. I take a deep breath and wait while the manager introduces me. I hear some cheers and whistles from my crew upfront and I step onto the stage. The lights dim as I make my way to the center of the stage and then step behind the microphone stand. I lower it just a bit, place my hands around the microphone and feel a spotlight illuminate my face. Nearby, the pianist begins to play the notes of my first song.

*Here we go,* I think.

Everything falls away and the only thing I'm aware of is the music and my voice. It's like all other sound and movement ceases and I'm transported to another time and place. The music takes over and it's like I blackout.

I can't see anyone in the crowd because the light shines in my eyes, but I feel my friends are nearby supporting me. And, it's a wonderful thing. My set moves quickly and each song flows from my mouth with ease.

Before I know it, I'm starting my last song and the room seems completely silent. But, I'm still in my own little world as I quietly begin singing, "I'm a fool to want you. I'm a fool to want you. To want a love that can't be true. A love that's there for others too."

The music feels like a living, breathing creature as I sing and the accompanying piano music is slow, sad and full of emotion. Just like my voice. And, when I reach the final verse, you could hear a pin drop. "I'm a fool to want you. Pity me, I need you. I know it's wrong, it must be wrong. But right or wrong I can't get along...Without you."

As the last note fades away, I open my eyes and realize tears stream down my face. The entire club bursts into applause and my table of friends hoot, holler and yell loudest of all. "Thank you," I say and then walk off the stage.

Once I'm safely in the shadows backstage, I release a shaky breath and lean a hand against the wall. *I did it. I really did it.* And, I think they must have liked me because the audience is still clapping.

I only wish Ryan was here.

# Chapter Eighteen: Ryan

When Saturday evening arrives, I know I should be at the Magnolia Club to support Hailey. Instead, I'm on a date with Daphne, the woman I met online and who I finally agreed to meet.

And, it's a disaster.

Not overtly because we have some things in common and the conversation flows smoothly enough. But, because I can't stop thinking about Hailey. I keep looking at my watch, ready to call it a night, wondering if I should try to still make Hailey's gig.

But, why would I do that? So, I can run into Bella? Create a big scene and ruin Hailey's night? No, I won't do that to her.

The minute we finish eating, I request the check. I see Daphne raise her brow and I sigh. "I'm sorry," I say. "You're a very nice woman, but I can't do this."

"Do what?" she asks. "Eat dinner?"

My mouth edges up. "You're right. I know this is just a first date and all, but I've got a lot going on and it's probably best if I focus on that right now."

"I'm not asking to marry you, Ryan, but I understand. Take care of your business and follow your heart. It's all any of us can do, right?"

On the drive back to Sunset Terrace, I ponder Daphne's parting words. *Follow your heart.* My heart leads me straight to Hailey. And, all I've been doing, since the moment I met her, is fighting it. Fighting me feelings, denying myself, pretending I'd be better off without her.

I pull up alongside the building, get out of my truck and head toward my apartment.

"Ryan?"

I look over and see Paige sitting by the pool. *What is my ex-wife doing here?* I wonder. I walk over and feel panic fill my gut. "Is Bella okay?" I ask, worry furrowing my brow.

Paige stands up. "She's fine." I wait for Paige to explain her visit, but she doesn't seem sure how to start. "It's been awhile."

"It's been more than awhile," I say and we both give each other a tentative smile. "You look great, by the way." And, she does. The years have been kind and I sense a happiness in her that was always missing when we were together.

"Thank you," she says, eyes roaming over me. "And, you look handsome, as always." Paige takes a deep breath and sits back down.

I slowly lower myself down on the chaise lounge next to her and frown. "What's going on?"

"I talked to Bella the other day. She said you two had a really good conversation and then told me everything. And, I guess I just wanted to come over and apologize."

I just blink, not sure what she means. "For what?"

"For all the years I let you be the bad guy." She shrugs. "I know it wasn't right, placing all of the blame on you, and I see that now. After your lunch, Bella started asking me questions about when we were married and I was brutally honest. For once, I didn't make it sound like I was completely innocent in the situation."

For a moment, I have no words. Then, I clear my throat. "I appreciate that. I hate that she's always thought of me as the villain and the reason we got divorced."

"I suppose I did it to punish you and it was wrong. I told her what a good man you are and I hope she can see that and not be swayed by what I've said over the years. Because I've spent so much of that time as a very bitter and miserable woman."

When tears shimmer in her eyes, I feel bad. Even though I'm the one who has had to deal with her little white lies. "She said you met someone recently."

A smile curves her mouth and Paige nods. "I guess it's true when they say love has the power to change people. Because I've never been happier."

"Good for you, Paige."

"What about you, Ryan?" She leans forward and touches my arm. "I can't believe that some woman hasn't come along and snatched you up. You've always been quite the catch."

"Since our divorce, I've avoided anything serious. I felt like a failure and decided it just wasn't worth it." I think of Hailey and how she made me want to try again. How we came so damn close.

"I'm sensing a 'but'…"

I release a weary sigh. "But, recently there was someone and it's like she turned the light on again for me."

"That's wonderful. Why do you say 'was,' though?"

"Because I ended it."

"Why?"

"There were too many complications."

Paige nods and clasps her hands in her lap. "Isn't that when it can be most exciting, though? When it's intense and there's something to fight for?"

Hailey is definitely worth fighting for and I wonder if I'm the world's biggest fool.

"Do you love her?" Paige asks.

My head snaps up and I feel liquid warmth flow through my veins like magma. *Yes,* I realize. I do love that sweet, innocent, young woman who ran away from an abusive uncle to pursue her dreams here. I admire her tenacity, bravery and, most of all, I love the fearless way she faces life head-on and goes after what she wants with such determination and strength.

I give a small nod. "But, I screwed it all up."

"So fix it. If you love her, then she's worth the risk."

"She's a lot younger than me, Paige," I admit and run a hand through my hair.

For a moment, Paige considers my words. "Why is that a bad thing? If you love her and she loves you, then you've been given a gift, Ryan. Don't throw it away because you're scared of what other people might think."

"I was terrified of what you and Bella would think," I tell her.

Paige gives me a smile and smacks my leg. "Oh, for God's sake, Ryan, you really haven't changed. You've always been the guy who tried to do the right thing and that's all very sweet, but, at some point, you need to put yourself first. It may sound selfish, but if it helps you find your happiness then do it. Be with the younger girl and don't give a damn about what anyone else thinks. Including me and Bella. Because, Rye, we'll support you no matter what."

*God.* I can't believe these words are coming out of her mouth and, for the first time in years, I feel a weight lift off my shoulders. Paige is right. I've spent my whole life making sure everyone else was happy and taken care of and somewhere along the way, I sacrificed my own wants and needs.

I glance down at my watch and realize I might have just enough time to catch Hailey's performance. I jump up and feel a huge smile on my face. "Thank you, Paige. But, I gotta go."

She stands up and laughs as I start jogging away. "Where are you going?"

"To go get my girl."

I race over to the Magnolia Club in record time and run through the front door. As I pay a small cover charge, I can hear Hailey's voice. It fills the air, sweet and melancholy. Literally, the most beautiful sound I have ever heard. As usual, her voice draws me forward, yet I stay in the back of the club and watch from the corner.

Hailey sounds like an angel and I look over everyone in the club. Conversations have stopped and they're mesmerized, their complete attention on her. When Hailey sings, she commands the room. It's an amazing thing to see.

Nearby, I notice a man in a dress shirt and tie talking on his phone in an excited whisper. "Are you hearing this?" He holds up his phone. "She's fucking the next big thing. Hell, yeah, I'm going to sign her. She's going to be famous."

His words make me smile, but also a little sad. This is exactly what she hoped would happen. Someone important in the music Industry would hear her and help launch her career. I'm so happy for her, but the reality of the situation leaves me cold. Because where would I fit in? I'm just an older man with baggage who owns an apartment complex. Hailey will be surrounded by people and be too busy for me.

Even though I came here prepared to fight for her, I know deep down it's best to let her go. Seeing her in her element makes me see that I have no place in her life.

The moment she finishes her set, the crowd goes wild and the walls shake from the raucous applause. Hailey murmurs a thank you and exits the stage. I clap so hard my hands hurt. I'm so damn proud of her.

Just when I'm debating whether or not to sneak back out, I suddenly notice a man who looks a little rough around the edges. He leans against the wall, arms crossed and not applauding.

In fact, he looks downright angry and I feel a prickle along the back of my neck. Something about him is off and I decide I am not going anywhere. Instead, I keep my eyes on him. From being in the military, I've learned to spot a bad guy a mile away.

And, this is a bad guy.

As the lights in the room lift, people start talking again and glasses clink as they finish their drinks. I plan to melt back into the shadows and keep vigilance for a while when I hear Bella's voice, loud and clear and very close.

"Dad? What are you doing here?"

I turn and see Bella, Hailey and a whole group of kids from Sunset Terrace. *Shit.* This is not how I expected Bella would find out about Hailey.

"You came?"

Hailey's soft voice snags my attention and I smile. "I wouldn't miss it for the world," I tell her. "And, you were absolutely amazing."

"Thank you," she whispers and, for a long moment, we just look at each other and it's as though no one else is in the room.

Then, everything becomes chaotic. The music Industry guy in the tie descends on Hailey like a shark and Bella gives me an unreadable look.

"Dad!"

I turn my attention to Bella, preparing for the wrath that I feel is about to come. I also notice that she wears the heart necklace I gave her. Even though it's gold and she prefers silver.

"How do you know Hailey?" she asks, hands on her hips.

"Uh-oh," Jasmine says under her breath. Then, she directs the group away from Bella and I, giving us some privacy. "Why don't we go over to the bar and get a drink?" she suggests.

"She lives at Sunset Terrace." I take a deep breath and then spill it. "And, we've been seeing each other."

Bella's eyes widened. "Are you shitting me?"

"Isabella-"

"She's *my* age!"

"I know that and I understand this is a shock to you, but please understand when I tell you that it's more than just a fling. I care about her...so much." I want to say that I love her, but I should probably let Hailey know that first.

"This is so weird." She shakes her head, trying to process it. "I can't deal with this right now." Bella turns to leave and I grab her arm.

"Bella-"

"Not now, Dad." She pulls free and storms out.

*Fuck.* This is not what I wanted to happen.

# Chapter Nineteen: Hailey

*Ryan came. He's here.* It's all I can think about as the agent tries to pitch me on why I should sign with him. He promises me the stars, moon and a connection to every person of importance in the music Industry. It feels so good to be noticed and appreciated. I let him do his spiel and then I tell him I'm very interested. We set up a meeting for Monday morning and I'm thrilled.

But, even more so, I'm so happy that Ryan came to support me. I'm not sure where he went and I head for the door. I hope he's waiting for me outside because I desperately want to talk to him and clear the air once and for all. I need to know exactly how he feels and what he wants to do. Because it's pretty clear that his daughter knows about us now.

I draw in a deep breath of fresh air and suddenly freeze. My blood runs cold when I see my Uncle Wayne stands nearby in the parking lot, leaning against his beat-up truck. "Hailey-girl. Aren't you a sight for sore eyes?"

"What're you doing here?" I manage to ask. My voice sounds like a croak and the entire world feels like it's tilting. Fear slithers through my veins as he steps closer.

"What? Your Uncle Wayne can't come visit you?"

"No, you can't."

He shakes his shaggy head. "Always so high and mighty. You must really think you're special now, huh? Singin' in front of all those fancy people." He spits on the ground. "But, you're still the same little nobody from Indiana. Probably would do you some good to get knocked down a coupla pegs."

I can't move and terror holds me hostage as my uncle moves closer. "Stay away from me. I don't want anything to do with you."

"Seems 'bout right since you ran off in the middle of the night without so much as a by-your-leave."

"I don't need your permission."

"You always were an ungrateful brat," he says and lifts his hand. His palm is big and callused and I know how hard he can hit. I cringe, close my eyes and wait for the force of his blow to hit me.

But, it never comes.

Something rushes past me and the slight breeze lifts my hair. Then, I hear my uncle grunt and I open my eyes. Ryan throws another punch that catches my uncle in the jaw and he literally spins. I gasp, cover my mouth and watch as Ryan hits him repeatedly. Until, he drops to the ground and covers his head from the blows.

"Ryan!" I cry. But, it's as though he doesn't hear me. He's so laser-focused on beating my uncle into the pavement that I have to reach out and grab his arm. "Ryan, stop."

Breathing hard, chest heaving, Ryan turns and I've never seen such a savage look on his face. "Are you okay?" he asks and grabs my shoulders.

I nod, still trying to reconcile the sweet manager of Sunset Terrace with the ferocious protector in front of me who just kicked the crap out of my abuser. He pulls me into his arms, lets out a relieved sigh and presses a kiss to my head. I wrap my arms around him and bury my face in his warm chest. "Thank you," I murmur.

He pulls back, touches a finger to the scar at the corner of my eye. "He's never going to hurt you again. I'll make sure of it." His green eyes flash and a shiver runs through me.

"Who the hell are you?" my uncle demands as he drags himself up off the ground.

"I'm the one who's going to make sure you never come near Hailey again. You don't contact her, you don't approach her, you don't even dare to breathe the same air as her. Because if you do, I will hunt you down and you will fucking disappear. Got it?"

For the first time ever, my uncle looks scared.

"She owes me," he whines.

"She owes you shit," Ryan snaps. "Now get the hell out of here before I finish what I started. Because, trust me, I'd like nothing more than to hurt you for all the pain you've put her through."

"You touch me again and I'll call the-"

Ryan lunged at him and my uncle yelped and hurried back to his truck. Then, Ryan smoothed my hair back and pressed a kiss to my lips. "He's never going to bother you again. I promise."

No one has ever stood up for me like Ryan and my heart tightens. When tears prick my eyes, he moves his thumbs to the corners of my eyes and wipes them away.

"Don't cry, sweetheart. You did so great and I am so damn proud of you."

A throat clears and Ryan and I look over and see Bella standing there. I don't know how long she's been there and I'm still in the circle of Ryan's arms. I take a step back and have no idea what to say.

Ryan drops his lips to my ear. "Give me a second, sweetheart." When I move to walk away, he grabs my hand. "But, stay with me. Right where you belong."

His words fill me with hope and love.

Bella looks from me to him, seemingly at a loss for words.

"Isabella, I know this is a bit of a shock, but I hope you can accept the fact that Hailey and I care for each other and want to be together." He lifts my hand and presses a kiss to its back.

"I don't know what to say," Bella finally says. "I'm just a little surprised."

*Of course, she is*, I think. And, it's to be expected. I just pray that this doesn't destroy the fragile relationship that these two have. I know it's Ryan's biggest fear and all I want to do is set her mind at ease.

"I didn't know you were Ryan's daughter," I admit. "He always referred to you as Bella so I didn't make the connection. But, I just want you to know how much I appreciate your friendship. It means the world to me, Isa. And, Ryan also means the world to me. I would never do anything to hurt him or you. I love him. Very much."

Bella's face softens and Ryan looks down at me. "You love me?" he asks.

I nod and feel a flush creep over my face.

A smile lights up his handsome face. "Good. Because I love you, too, and I'm never letting you go."

"Promise?"

Ryan kisses the tip of my nose. "Promise."

I realize Bella is watching us closely and I'm not sure what is running through her head. I just mentally cross my fingers and hope for the best.

"You know," Bella begins and places her hands on her hips, "this is probably a good thing."

Ryan keeps an arm around my waist and we wait for her to continue.

"For a couple of reasons," she says. "First of all, you've been alone for a really, really long time, Dad."

I smirk and Ryan quirks a brow. "Sad, but true," he says.

"And, I've seen how finding someone and falling in love has changed Mom. It's made her so happy. And, I want that for you, too." Bella turns her attention to me. "And, Hailey, I just love you to death. If you make each other happy…then I'm happy for you."

I hear Ryan release a breath. "Thanks, honey."

God, I'm so relieved to hear her words.

"There's one other thing," Bella says, suddenly looking sheepish.

"What?" Ryan asks.

"So, you know how I started dating this guy recently?"

We both nod.

"Well, he's a little older than me."

Suddenly, I know exactly where this is going and I bite my lip to keep from laughing. Oh, poor Ryan. Talk about karma.

"How much older?" Ryan asks.

"That's not really the point," I say and reach for his hand. "Are you happy?"

Bella nods. "We're in love and I haven't told anyone yet because of our age difference. But, now that I have such a good example…"

I press my lips together, trying to hold the chuckle in, but it escapes. "Well, I look forward to meeting him and I'm sure your father does, too."

Ryan lets out a little groan, but forces a smile. "I certainly do."

"Oh, good!" Bella says and claps her hands together. "Mom doesn't have any idea so don't say anything. I'm going to need you to help me tell her."

Bella walks over and she and Ryan hug.

"I'm so glad you understand, Dad. We're going to have to figure out a way to tell Mom without giving her a mini heart attack."

"A heart attack is a bit of a strong reaction. Even for your Mom."

"How many years are you and Hailey apart?" she asks.

I twirl a strand of hair around my finger, highly amused, and decide not to comment.

"Twenty years," he says.

"Oh, okay. That's not too bad."

From the look on Ryan's face, I think he may have just had a little heart attack. But, for the first time in a long time, he gets to be a dad to his daughter. And, I know he likes that. Even if it's killing him a little.

We start to walk to our cars and Ryan finally asks, "So, how many years exactly are you and this guy apart?"

"Just a few more than you two." She links an arm through his and smiles. "Who knew we had so much in common?"

His mouth opens, then closes. *My adorable Foxy Flyboy is at a loss for words.*

But, I have a feeling that his future relationship with his daughter will be a strong one.

# Chapter Twenty: Ryan

Hailey, Bella and I decide to go out to dinner and the amazing thing is it feels right, normal and not awkward like I had always feared it would be. Bella is so accepting of us and maybe a part of it is because she's dating an older man, but who am I to judge?

At the moment, everything feels perfect. Like when I took Hailey flying. Short of a nuclear war or an alien invasion, I don't think anything could put a damper on our happiness. It's been so long since I've felt like this.

Hell, who am I kidding? I've never actually felt like this. The future is bright and I couldn't be more ready.

After dinner, we say goodbye to Bella and Hailey invites her and her man to the pool party/ barbecue tomorrow. I figure it's best I meet this new beau of hers sooner than later since now I've been roped into helping break the news to her mother.

*Good times, being a father,* I think with a little smile.

When we get back to Sunset Terrace, it's dark and quiet. After all the craziness earlier, it's nice to be back home. I take Hailey's hand and guide her over to my place. I don't plan on letting her leave until tomorrow because tonight, I have all sorts of steamy plans for her.

I close the door behind us and pull her into my arms. She smiles, but I can tell her mind is elsewhere. "What?" I ask and run a hand through her long, dark hair.

"You don't think my uncle will be back do you?"

I can hear the worry in her voice, see the fear in her big, brown eyes, and I hate it. "No. I'll make sure he never bothers you again. You have nothing to worry about, Hailey." The fact that he hurt her is like a knife digging into my heart. It makes me sick. The tip of my index finger touches the crescent scar by the corner of her eye. "You're safe, sweetheart."

"I suppose I'm worthless to him now, anyway. All he cared about was my virginity."

"And, that's mine," I growl and pull her against me. I lower my head and capture her lips in a slow, possessive kiss. When my tongue glides into her mouth, she responds back with hers. After a minute of feasting on her sweetness, I pull back, scoop her up into my arms and carry her down to my bedroom.

"And, you're not worthless," I tell her.

Very slowly, I lower her down, her lithe body dragging down the length of mine. Then, my hands reach around and lower the zipper on her dress. It drops in a midnight pile around her feet and my gaze lowers to admire the lace bra and panties. "You're so beautiful," I whisper and run a hand up her side. I can smell the gardenia still tucked behind her ear mixed in with her warm vanilla scent.

She lets out a little gasp as my palm curves around her breast and she pushes into my hand. Her fingers start to work the buttons down on my shirt and then she slips it off my shoulders.

"You're beautiful, too," she whispers and runs her hands over my chest. "So strong, so powerful." She drops kisses along my pecs and my breath hitches when her hands drop and caress down the front of my pants. "So big."

"Naughty girl," I say, instantly hard as steel.

She gives me a wicked smile and then leans over to take off her strappy high heels. But, I grab her arm and pull her back up.

"Leave them on," I tell her in a low voice.

Hailey looks down at my pants. "Only if you take those off," she says with a sexy, little smile.

I rip my pants and boxer briefs off in one fell swoop and push into her. We fall back onto the bed and I ravish her mouth in a kiss that's deep, demanding and full of so much desire that it's a little scary. I've never wanted anyone this much in my life.

Hailey responds back like always-- with so much enthusiasm and vigor that it riles me up even more. "Ryan," she moans and undulates against me. "I need you inside me."

I grind my pelvis up against her in answer and then reach down and yank the tiny bit of lace off her lower body. The bra follows and I let my mouth trail over her, starting at her temple then moving down to her lips sliding along her neck, breasts and stomach. I pause and look up as she writhes, hands clenching the blanket.

"What do you need, sweetheart? Tell me."

"Your mouth," she rasps.

"Where? Show me."

Hailey drops her hand between her thighs and I follow with my mouth, ready to grant her every desire.

"Oh, God, Ryan," she cries.

I don't hold back and devour her. When I suck that sweet, little bud between my lips and rub it with my tongue, I know she's ready to explode. I know she's throbbing just like I am.

But, I pull away and Hailey lets out a moan of protest. "You're going to come on my cock, little nightingale."

She props herself up on an elbow, watching as I grab a condom. "Nightingale?" She smirks.

I move back between her legs, spreading her thighs, and position myself at the juncture where she's wet and ready. "Yeah, my little songbird who would sing at night and tease me. Keep me up, listening, wanting, needing you."

Her face flushes and her hands run down my back. "Fill me up, Ryan. Now."

I push into her and she arches beneath me with a sigh. She wraps her legs around me and digs the points of her high heels into the backs of my thighs. God, she's so sexy and she doesn't even know it. Need washes over me and I pick the pace up, sliding in and out of her, fast and hard. *Mine. Hailey Aurora Lane is all mine.*

I reach down between our slick bodies and press her clit until she's convulsing around me, drawing me deeper. A shaky cry erupts from her throat, she screams my name as her entire body tightens and then collapses.

I'm a second behind her and my climax slams into me harder than ever. The pressure that's been building explodes like a Fourth of July fireworks finale and I rise up on my elbows and shudder with a release that leaves me breathless and completely spent.

After I drop down beside her, I reach over and fix the gardenia that's slipping from behind her ear. "I'm not going to let anyone hurt you ever again. I'll always keep you safe."

"I haven't felt safe since my parents died."

"With me, you'll always be safe. Whatever you want, whatever you need, I'll be. Your Daddy, your partner, your lover, your best friend. I want to be everything to you because I love you. So damn much."

"Ryan…" She lays a hand against the side of my face and I pull her closer.

"I'm so sorry that I pushed you away when all I wanted was to be with you. I convinced myself that you were better off without me, but I never stopped wanting you, Hailey. I'll never stop needing you, little songbird. Never."

I kiss her long and slow. And, the moment she melts into me, it's like pure heaven.

"I love you, Ryan," she whispers. "And, whatever you need, I'll be. Your little girl, your nightingale, your lover, your best friend."

Emotion washes through me and I know that I've been blessed with a rare second chance at love. And, this is a love that's more powerful than any I've known before.

There's no doubt in my mind that I am the luckiest man in the world.

# Epilogue: Hailey

Waking up in Ryan's bed, snuggled up in his arms, my head lays against his chest and I listen to his strong heartbeat. A heart that is also so kind and full of love. And, I'm so happy to know that this amazing man is finally all mine.

We didn't get much sleep last night and I yawn, pull back and stretch. For the first time since I can remember, everything feels right in my world. I don't feel scared or worried or hurt. The edginess that used to plague me is gone. I'm not afraid that I'm going to see my Uncle Wayne again, thanks to Ryan. In fact, after getting a taste of his own medicine, I am confident that he is out of my life for good.

"Morning," Ryan says, his voice rough with sleep.

I reach over and lay my hand on his chest. "Morning."

He instantly reaches up and covers my hand with his. "Sorry, I didn't let you get much sleep last night," he says with a smirk.

"I'm not."

"Yeah, I'm actually not, either," he says and gives a low, husky laugh.

"So, are you ready to meet Bella's boyfriend today?"

He lets out a breath and squeezes my hand. "Is a Dad ever ready to meet his daughter's boyfriend?"

I chuckle. "She's got you between a rock and a hard place, you know."

"I know, but hopefully he's a good man. I think being with you has expanded my horizons a little, you know?"

"Oh, I'll expand your horizons, alright," I say and pinch his nipple.

"You're something else, you know that?"

"And, you love it."

"I do." He slaps my ass and I give a little squeal and hop out of bed. After I use the bathroom and wash my face, Ryan comes in and hands me an extra toothbrush. He squeezes some toothpaste on it and then his. As we brush our teeth, side by side, I look at our reflection in the mirror and love this feeling. I bump his hip with mine.

"I could get used to this," I say and spit into the sink. I rinse my mouth and watch him finish up.

"Get used to what?" he asks and reaches for a can of shaving cream.

"Sharing the bathroom with you every morning."

He slathers the cream over his lower face and lifts a razor.

"Watching you shave." I hop up on the counter, fascinated by the way he moves the blade over his face with practiced ease.

"Is it really that exciting?" he asks and raises a brow.

"I think so."

He leans over the sink, splashes his face with water and I watch how his broad back ripples with each movement. Heat fills me. Then, he stands back upright, grabs a towel and wipes his face off.

Ryan glances over and I must be pretty easy to read because he moves over between my legs, grasps my hips and pulls me forward. "I didn't know shaving turned you on this much," he whispers.

"Everything about you turns me on, Foxy Flyboy."

His lips twitch. "That's such a ridiculous nickname."

"You know you love it."

He leans down and gives me a very long, very thorough pepperminty kiss.

"How about showers? Those turn you on, too?" He tugs me off the counter with a devilish smile. "Because we can share that every morning, too."

I bite the inside of my cheek as he guides me over to the large, stand-up shower and turns the water on. Yes, I think, I could easily get used to a life with Ryan Fox.

Later that afternoon we sit on the couch and watch a movie. Ryan must be thinking he could get used to living with me, too, because he turns to me and I can feel his serious green gaze.

"What?" I ask.

"I was just thinking about what you said earlier," he begins slowly. His fingers snake through mine. "I know it's fast, but…what do you think about moving in with me?"

I crawl up into his lap and gaze into those beautiful minty-green eyes of his. "You sure you want me living here?"

"I want you as close to me as possible, all of the time, my little songbird."

A huge smile lights my face up and I nod vehemently.

He laughs. "Is that a yes?"

"A million percent, it's a yes!"

As we kiss, it amazes me how fast my life has changed. I left Indiana in the middle of the night, a scared, lonely, abused girl with no one to turn to and only with the slim hope that I could start a life in Los Angeles. And, of course, a dream in my heart.

And, now here I am, in the arms of the most extraordinary man I've ever met who loves me and will protect me. I'm so happy, so blessed and I'm practically bursting at the seams.

"You know, I just finished unpacking, too," I lament.

He gives me a devastating smile. "Well, pack it all right back up, baby. Because I'm moving you in this week."

The pool party and barbecue tonight is more fun than ever before. Everyone congratulates me on my performance at the Magnolia Club and wishes me luck with the meeting that I have tomorrow with the agent.

"Tomorrow at this time, you're going to have representation!" Jasmine announces. "I'm so happy for you, Hailey."

"You know what that means?" Taylor adds. "We need another girls' night out to celebrate because our friend is on her way to becoming a mega-big superstar!"

"One step at a time," I say and laugh. I love all of their support and I am so happy to have these girls in my life.

"I'm going to make everyone I know download your album," Jasmine promises.

The funny thing is, I know she's not kidding.

"We'll make sure you go platinum," Taylor says with a wink.

A moment later, I feel Ryan's arms slide around my waist and I tilt my head back and give him a smile. "What's going on, ladies?" he asks and presses a kiss to my temple.

Jasmine and Taylor collectively sigh. Then, Jasmine puts her hands on her hips. "I can't believe you told him his nickname."

"Sorry, Jazz. But, I thought he should know how the women of Sunset Terrace really feel."

I think it's adorable when a blush rises in his cheeks.

"Well, I'm glad you two are finally together," Taylor says. "You're a perfect match."

"Thanks, Tay," I say. "I think so, too."

"Though, I have to say the pool fight was quite entertaining," Jasmine comments with an innocent look.

I stifle a laugh and Ryan just shakes his head.

When a car pulls up at the curb, we all look over to see Bella and a tall man with sandy-colored hair get out. I notice the way he walks around the car and opens the door for her. And, I'm pretty sure Ryan does, too.

"Very polite," I whisper and Ryan only grunts. "Remember, keep an open mind and be nice."

"I'm always nice," he says.

"C'mon," I say and grab his hand.

Bella and her boyfriend head up the walkway and we meet them halfway up. For a nervous moment, we all look at each other. Then, Ryan extends his hand. "I'm Ryan, Isabella's Dad."

"Good to meet you, Ryan," he says. "I'm Shawn Cullin."

Shawn looks to be around Ryan's age, early 40s, and I can tell that he's nervous. He swipes a hand through his short, sandy hair and clears his throat.

"This is Hailey," Ryan says, introducing me.

"Hello," I say with a smile, reach over and shake his hand.

"Thanks for inviting us over, Dad," Bella says and toys with the gold heart necklace around her neck. "It means a lot," she adds under her breath.

Ryan gives Bella a hug. "You're always welcome here, honey." He turns his attention back to Shawn. "We have a barbecue by the pool every Sunday and you both have a standing invitation."

Bella smiles and reaches for Shawn's hand. "Thanks, Dad."

"Why don't we get you both a cold drink," I suggest.

We all head for the cooler that sits near the grill. While Bella and Shawn choose a drink, Ryan lifts the lid on the grill and flips the burgers and hotdogs.

"So, how did you two meet?" I ask.

"Remember when I flew to New York a couple of months ago?" Bella asks Ryan.

"To visit your friend," Ryan says.

"Yeah. Well, I met Shawn at the airport while I was waiting for my connecting flight," Bella says. "Didn't I tell you he's a pilot?"

Ryan's head snaps up and I feel a smile tug at the corner of my mouth.

"No, you didn't mention that. You fly?" he asks, attention on Shawn.

"I do. I became a commercial airline pilot after I retired from the Air Force."

*Bull's eye,* I think. There is no doubt in my mind that this is the beginning of a beautiful friendship.

"No shit," Ryan says. "I was 160th."

"Really? That's incredible. I actually thought about trying to do that, but that's a tough job."

"Brutal, but I loved it. I just took Hailey flying last week."

"You went flying?" Bella asks.

I nod. "It was so much fun."

"What did you pilot?" Shawn asks.

"My friend Jax owns a Robinson R44 that I use."

"Oh, man, a Raven I? How does she handle?"

"Like a dream. Four-seater, 260 hp carbureted Lycoming 6-cylinder engine and hydraulically assisted flight controls."

"The flight controls are directly linked by pulleys and push-pull rods?"

"That's right."

I turn to Bella and smile. "This could go on for a while," I say.

She laughs.

"C'mon, let's go sit in the sun with Jazz and Taylor while they talk shop."

It's not long before the Dynamic Duo graces us with their presence by doing cannonballs into the pool. Mason and Cody manage to splash us, but it feels good and we all laugh. I look over and see that Ryan and Shawn are deep in conversation, most likely about helicopters or planes. It's pretty cute.

I take a sip of my soda and look around at all of my new friends. Morgan is missing and I assume she's working like usual. And, Jazz said Savannah and Nick decided to head out of town for one last trip alone before she's too far along to fly. I know they're excited to welcome their twin girls and I look forward to meeting them.

But, a little alone time is always a wonderful thing, I think, as I look over and study Ryan's handsome face. He must feel my gaze because he glances up. The moment our eyes lock, an electrical current flashes between us and I cross my legs, feeling a wave of anticipation. I have a feeling that we're going to be leaving the pool party early today.

"Hailey?"

"Hmm?"

"I asked if you and Ryan are official now?" Mason asks, sitting down next to Jasmine. She makes a face as he drips water all over her lounge chair.

I glance over at Bella. "Actually, I'm going to be moving in with him."

To my relief and happiness, she gives me a small smile. "If you need any help moving, let me know."

"Thank you," I say. I have a feeling that Bella and I are going to become very close. Like sisters, and I couldn't be more excited.

Cody whistles. "What is it with apartment 12?"

"What do you mean?" I ask and turn to look up at him, shading my eyes from the bright sun.

"Isn't it obvious? Whoever moves into that place falls in love and moves out within a month."

Jasmine raises a brow. "You know, I think you're right. First Savvy, now Hailey. Who's next?"

We all look at Taylor who shifts on her lounge chair. "Why is everyone looking at me?" she asks, blue eyes wide. She gives her red hair a shake and crosses her arms. "I have no time for a man in my life. I'm far too busy with ballet and working until 2am every night. Maybe you should move in there, Jazz."

"Oh, hell, no," she says. "I'm barely around as it is. I think it's much better-suited for you, Tay."

Taylor gives a huff. "I'm quite comfortable where I am, thank you very much."

We all laugh and then Ryan calls us over because the food is ready. I fill my plate with chips, some macaroni salad and wait for a hotdog. Bella is second to last in line, just ahead of me, and she pauses.

"How's it going between you and Shawn?" I hear her ask in a low voice.

"I like him," Ryan says. "I think your Mom will, too."

All of a sudden, Bella throws her arms around Ryan in a fierce hug. "Love you, Dad," she whispers.

I see Ryan's eyes slide shut and I can only imagine how long he's been waiting to hear those words from her and how much they must mean to him. "Love you, too, Bella-Vanilla," he says in a voice tight with emotion.

After Bella walks away to join Shawn by the pool, I move up beside Ryan and lay a hand along his dear face. "Are you okay?"

It takes him a moment to collect himself, but then he nods. "I've never been better."

"I'm glad."

He lets out a shaky breath and places a hotdog in the bun on my plate.

"Smells delicious," I tell him. "And, it looks like you and Shawn have a few things in common."

His mouth edges up. "Maybe a couple things," he admits. "From what I can tell, he seems like a good guy. I'm sure Paige will like him just as much as I do."

"Hopefully he doesn't remind her too much of you," I tease.

"Hey!" He nudges me with an elbow.

"I told everyone we were moving in together this week."

"What did Bella say?" he asks.

"She offered to help me," I announce.

I see the happiness in his eyes and he nods. "I think everything is going to work out just fine, Hailey Aurora Lane." He takes my plate, sets it on the side of the grill and pulls me into his arms.

I let out a content sigh. "I think you're right, Foxy Flyboy."

"Oh, God," he grumbles. "I'm never going to hear the end of that, am I?"

I chuckle. "Nope. Because that's exactly what you are-- a dashing pilot who flew into my life like an absolute whirlwind and stole my heart."

"And, your virginity," he adds with a wicked smile and nips my bottom lip.

"No," I say and wrap my arms around his neck. "That was my gift to you."

I look deeply into his light green eyes and know that we have a beautiful future ahead of us and I am so excited to start it together.

"I love you, little songbird."

"Love you, too."

Then, his lips capture mine and my stomach drops. And, once again, it feels like I'm soaring through the skies again with my Foxy Flyboy.

Printed in Great Britain
by Amazon